Peter Corris was born in Victoria, but is now an enthusiastic resident of Sydney, which has provided the locale for his other Cliff Hardy stories. He was originally a historian, but would now classify himself as a journalist and thriller writer.

THE
Greenwich Apartments

Peter Corris

UNWIN PAPERBACKS
Sydney London Boston

First published in Australia
by Unwin Paperbacks 1986

UNWIN ® PAPERBACKS
Allen & Unwin Australia Pty Ltd
8 Napier St, North Sydney NSW 2060 Australia

Allen & Unwin New Zealand Limited
60 Cambridge Terrace, Wellington, New Zealand.

UNWIN PAPERBACKS
18 Park Lane, Hemel Hempstead Herts HP2 4TE England

© Peter Corris 1986

National Library of Australia
Cataloguing-in-Publication entry:
Corris, Peter, 1942-   .
   The Greenwich apartments.

   ISBN 0 04 820030 1.

   I. Title.

A823'.3

Typeset in Century Schoolbook by Setrite Typesetting
Hong Kong
Printed by The Dominion Press-Hedges & Bell
Maryborough, 3465

Book One

FOR
Stephen Knight

1

THE building that went by the name of the Greenwich Apartments was a small block of flats, six two-bedroomers on three storeys, in behind a lively section of Bayswater Road, Kings Cross. To get to the flats I'd passed a brasserie and a restaurant and a wine bar. It was 9 p.m. and all three places were full. Someone had told me once which was the most trendy and hardest to get a table at, which was the next most desirable and which finished third, but I couldn't remember the sequence. Beside the entrances to the building that weren't places to eat and drink at, there were a couple of medicos' nameplates, discreet neon signs advertising massage, and even a plaque for a fellow practitioner—Terry Stafford, Private Inquiries. Never heard of him.

The traffic was heavy and the area was parked solid. There were cars in 'No Standing' zones and across driveways. It was as if everybody in Sydney wanted to pack into this couple of acres. I walked up a lane into a bricked courtyard in front of the flats. Light-coloured brick with dark trim around the windows; decent-sized balconies on the second and third levels. Ivy or something like it crawled up the front of the building and had got a grip on a couple of the balconies. It snaked up a drainpipe towards the roof. No graffiti, no broken windows. A nice place.

The courtyard was boxed in on all sides; lights showed in the other apartment buildings on two sides. The wall behind me was blank—back of a

3

hotel, possibly. No lights showed in the Greenwich Apartments. I stood in approximately the spot where Carmel Wise had been shot dead ten days before.

Here and there bricks were missing or had crumbled and some weeds had sprouted. There were plane trees for shade and a bench to sit on; there was a drinking fountain and a bicycle rack. There was a low pedestal in the middle of the square where a plastic and glass illuminated sign carrying the name of the place had been mounted. It was taken away after the bullets that hadn't hit Carmel Wise had smashed it. Maybe some of the bullets had hit the girl *and* the sign; I hadn't mastered all the exact details yet because Leo Wise had only hired me a few hours before. Leo Wise was Carmel's father. He also owned the block of flats.

'The Greenwich Apartments, it's called,' he'd said that afternoon. 'Not too far from here. Maybe you know it?'

I shook my head. I've had my office in St Peter's Lane for more than twelve years (I'd stopped counting at twelve), a stone's throw from the Cross, but my work tends to take me out of the area. I could name a few nearby pubs but no blocks of flats. 'No, afraid not,' I said 'is that why you came to me? For my local knowledge? If so, I'm sorry, I . . .'

He leaned forward. A big man, 50 plus with a heavy, forceful face and a manner to match. Expensive clothes, expensive teeth, not much hair and no nonsense. 'I'm a bereaved man, Hardy. I don't show it. I don't go around crying. I go to work and get on with it but I feel just as bad as . . .'

'As who?' I said.

'As her mother!' He banged my desk with his fist: my notebook shifted and a little dust lifted and settled. There was nothing else on the desk.

'I understand what you mean.'

4

'You'd have seen the reports in the a paper . . . of Carmel getting shot.' His mouth twisted bitterly. 'Everybody's seen them. That's one of the worst things.'

'I read something. She was twenty-one, I think it said. I don't remember her job. No motive.'

'She was a videotape editor and a filmmaker. Serious work. That didn't stop the crummy headlines. "Video Girl Slain in Cross". Crap!'

'I remember now. There were a couple of hundred videos in the flat . . .'

'Not one of them was a dirty movie. Not one!' The fist came down again. 'But the papers made it look as if they all were. Her mother's . . . bloody broken.' He stared through the dirty window. I've tried cleaning the windows inside but no-one is ever going to clean them outside—three floors up in Darling-hurst—so what's the point? He would have seen a bit of guttering hanging from the roof and the top of a church against a grey sky. I know because I've sat in the client's chair myself when business was slow, and pretended to be a client with an interesting case for me to handle. The fantasy has never taken me far; somehow it feels worse in the client's chair than in my own.

'The publicity stops,' I said. 'The police get on with it quietly.'

'There's things the police don't know,' he said. 'That's why I'm here. I'm told you can do a job and keep your mouth shut.'

'Yes,' I said.

'That's what I need. There's a strange angle on this, bloody strange. Anything about it in the papers'd probably send Moira, that's my wife, right around the bend. I'd end up with no wife as well as no daughter. The police talk to the reporters, every-one knows that. The reporters pay them.'

'Probably. I know a couple of cops who wouldn't

5

do that. I could have a word with them if you want.'

He shook his head. 'Can't risk it. Look, it could be nothing or it could lead into all sorts of shit. I just don't know. I'm not worried about myself. I've got nothing to hide.'

'Come on, Mr Wise. You're a businessman—investment consultant, did you say?'

His face was set grimly; it looked like the sort of face that could smile or cry it necessary, but only if he let it. 'What I've got to hide's hidden. And I've got no connections to any of this. Just . . . information.'

'Which you won't give to the police because you're worried about publicity.' I moved the notebook an inch to the right. 'It's thin, Mr Wise.'

'It's not thin, it's complicated. I want you to look into it, follow things up if you can, if there's anything to it . . .'

'Why?'

'To get whoever it was that killed Carmel.'

'Revenge,' I said. 'Trial. Publicity.'

'Carmel was an innocent bystander. With that clear I don't mind the publicity. It's all this "video girl" bullshit I can't handle. Please, Hardy, I need your help. What're your fees?'

'A hundred and twenty a day plus expenses.'

'Retainer?'

'Two days pay, up front.'

He got a cheque book from his inside jacket pocket. To get it he had to open the jacket. He was thick-bodied but not fat; he wore a white shirt and plain tie. There were sweat patches under his arms although the day was cool and his suit was lightweight. I sweat under pressure myself so I was sympathetic. He poised a ballpoint over the cheque.

'I'll give you a week in advance.'

'Easy,' I said. 'Give me the information you won't give the cops first. Then we'll see.'

6

The Greenwich Apartments, Leo Wise told me, were built in the 1930s when materials were plentiful and work was scarce.

'They're well-built, see? The builder could get the right timbers and everything and the workers wanted the job to last so they took care. I bought the place about three years ago. It was run-down of course, and two of the flats've been empty for a while. I'm . . . I was going to do them all up, eventually.'

'Uh huh.'

'So, numbers four and five, they're empty. There's a couple in number two, been there the whole time. And there's a young bloke in three. Agent reckons he's all right, pays on time.'

I wrote 'agent?' on a page of my notebook and waited for him to say more. He was looking out the window again. *Getting to the hard part*, I thought.

'Flat one's on the ground, right on ground level. No stairs or anything. You just walk in from the courtyard. Bugger all view, no balcony, smaller than the others if anything.'

He stopped again and it seemed like the time for me to say something. 'Do the tenants have leases?'

'What? Oh, no. Month to month. The place's got a few plumbing problems, roof's not too good. The rent's reasonable to take account of that. I wasn't rushing anybody. When they came vacant I just let them lie. I would've made some arrangements for anyone who was left when I wanted to get moving. I've got other places. Wouldn't have been any problem.'

I nodded, but he was going to need prompting. 'What about flat one, Mr Wise? What's the story?'

He sighed and stopped looking through the dirty glass. Another sigh and a rub of his hard jaw and he was ready to talk. 'That's the one Carmel was using.

7

She had a TV set there and her video collection.'

'Collection?'

'Yes. Old movies mostly. Foreign, a lot of them. It was her hobby as well as her work. She had a flat in Randwick but I suppose the videos took up too much space. Look, I'm not saying she was normal, but she wasn't a freak. She ...'

I clicked my tongue the way you do to soothe an angry dog. 'Okay, okay.'

He fought for control and got it. 'Right. Anyway, she asked me if she could use the flat and I said okay. Christ, I wish ...'

'I don't understand. This flat—what about it?'

'It's been vacant the whole time I've had the building.'

'Well, no difficulty then.'

'I shouldn't have done it. I shouldn't have let her use it and I meant to do something about it. I never did. Busy. You know how it is?'

'I'm not with you,' I said. 'Sounds like you didn't need the rent.'

'That's the point. The rent's been paid, on the knocker, every fortnight. Regular as clockwork and no-one ever spent a night there. Not for three years.'

2

I crossed the courtyard, ducking my head to avoid a plane tree branch, and pushed open the glass door that led to the small lobby and the stairway of the Greenwich Apartments. The lobby was dark, illuminated only by the light coming in from the courtyard through the door and the big window beside it. The floor was a concrete slab covered with lino tiles; there were no discernible smells. The letterboxes were set under the window. All six had light padlocks on the inside; none carried a name tag. The door to flat one was right in front of me, tucked in below the stairs, and I used the key Leo Wise had given me to open it.

I put my hand on the wall where a light switch should be and found it. The room I was in was small and made smaller by the stacks of video cassettes. They were in tiers on top of the TV set, in and on boxes, spilling over from collapsed piles into jumbled heaps on the carpet. A director's chair with red canvas seat and backing was lined up in front of the television set. There were cassettes on it as well. A VCR was on the floor beside the TV and a telephone sat on top of a pile of movies next to it.

I skirted around the plastic and carboard boxes and checked the other rooms—small bedroom, single bed, chest of drawers, built-in wardrobe (empty), more video cassettes, dozens of them, in and out of their boxes, all over the bed and around it on the floor. Kitchen—basic fittings, bar fridge, cupboards

9

empty apart from China tea, coffee (instant) and sugar. Bathroom—no bath, just a shower, hand-basin and toilet. Soap, towel, toilet-paper. No videos in the bathroom or kitchen. There were small windows in each room. Those from the bathroom and kitchen looked out into a kind of well, cluttered with plumbing and ventilation ducts, between this building and the next.

The window in the front room was covered with an old Holland blind. Suddenly, the light bulb hanging from the ceiling blew and the room went dark. I lifted the blind and felt the dry, old fabric crack and tear as it moved. It hadn't been lifted for a long time. Light from the courtyard where Carmel Wise had died seeped into the room.

I went into the bathroom, removed the bulb from the light fitting there and replaced the blown one in the front room. I took the boxes off the director's chair and sat down facing the TV. I sniffed the air. Dry, the flat didn't have any problems with damp which was no doubt good for the videos. No recent cooking or smoking but no recently opened windows either. No radio, no stereo, no old-time dance records. It looked as if all anyone had ever done in this place was watch the box, drink China tea and instant coffee and maybe talk on the telephone. It made no sense, there had to be more.

I got up and checked the rooms again. It was the cassettes that had thrown me off. Bright covers and dull; Gothic script and computer print; VHS, Super, Stereo 2000. They took all the attention. They made the mind wander off onto thoughts of Hollywood and J. Arthur Rank. But under the bed, down there with the dust and fluff, were three large, strapped-up and locked-tight suitcases. I dragged them out.

'If you're full of videos,' I said to them, 'I'm off the case.' It was a joke of a sort, better than no joke at all and I sniggered. The place was getting to me;

10

the plastic jumble offended my orderly mind. I liked the suitcases a lot better. I even liked them being locked. Professional skills to be called into play. Hardy earns his dough again.

Two of the suitcases were matched, the third was the odd man out—similar in size, good quality leather, slightly different in style. I started with that. The lock yielded easily to a small blade on my pocket knife. In Beirut you'd have to think about booby traps. This wasn't Beirut. I flipped open the lid and the mass of clothes and papers and books lifted as the pressure came off. I put the clothes—a man's jacket, several pairs of trousers, a couple of sweaters and shirts, socks, underwear, sandals and shoes—aside and looked at the other stuff. There were a couple of paper-back novels, some magazines, a pocket-sized spiral-bound notebook like my own, bills and receipts, bus and train tickets, the stubs of movie tickets, supermarket checkout dockets. The detritus of a modern city life but, as far as I could tell from a quick look, nothing with a name on it. There were also two fat manila envelopes, quarto size, filled with black and white photographs and negatives. Another manila envelope bulged with toothpaste, a toothbrush, shaving cream and a couple of disposable razors.

I examined the clothing. It would have fitted a man two inches smaller than me, say around five foot ten, and about a stone lighter, around eleven stone. It was all off the rack stuff, medium quality, worn but not worn out. There were no name tags, no laundry marks, and there was nothing in any of the pockets.

The matched cases would have been tougher to open; the locks were better made, with tricky sliding covers on them. But the keys were tied to the handles with light string. The first one I opened was full of women's clothes and shoes; the second contained more clothes plus a couple of handbags and purses. There were toilet articles, makeup, tampons, hairpins and all the other things that make a woman's bathroom cupboard different from a man's. The clothes were better quality than the man's; they had been worn less frequently and were better cared for. They were also more exotic.

I called them Mr and Mrs Greenwich in my imagination. Mr G. had nothing you couldn't buy and wear in Sydney; Mrs G. had some Thai silk scarves, some embroidered and beaded things that looked foreign, and a pale blue sari.

I got cramped squatting on the floor in the bedroom so I carried the handbags and purses and all the man's personal things out to the kitchen and put them on the table. The water was running and the gas was connected. Instant coffee, Cliff? Why not? Black? Fine. I sipped the coffee and dumped the contents of the purses out on the table. The woman was Mrs Greenwich no longer. She was Tania Hester Bourke, born Sydney, 6 May 1950, 168 centimetres tall, 55 kilos, brown hair, brown eyes, no visible scars. She had been licensed to drive in the state of New South Wales in 1980, had a Bankcard and an American Express card as befitted an Air Pacific hostess, and went to a dentist in Macquarie Street. All this came from the first and most obvious things I poked through. If I'd really dug I could probably have got to her HSC results and her first *Cosmo* subscription. There was a passport, cheque books, bank statements, parking tickets, the lot.

The coffee was foul. I emptied it into the sink and spread out a batch of the photographs. About half of the selection showed houses, boats and beaches without people—empty, deserted scenes probably caught in the early morning. The others were the exact opposite—people in rooms and on the same boats and beaches. People playing games, drinking,

12

talking. Nothing indiscreet. Maybe some of the cigarettes were more Griffith than Virginia but that's hardly a crime nowadays. One photograph showed a familiar face circled in red by a felt-tip pen. A woman's face, turned to the camera, one among a smiling group around a table. I turned the picture over; sure enough, that name again—'Tania', printed in block capitals with the same pen.

All this needed leisurely inspection. I could get Helen Broadway's opinion on the woman's things and perhaps get a lead on the man. I could try to identify the houses, boats and beaches. Lots to do, clues to follow, lives to construct. What I do best. I realised that it was getting late and that a drink would be welcome. Promising start, time to go. I could take some of the stuff with me and come back for the rest later. I found a green plastic garbage bag in the kitchen and dumped the handbags, a selection of the makeup, the photographs and Mr G.'s bits and pieces into it; folded up, I could easily carry it under one arm. I tossed in a pair of gold sandals with high heels and thin straps just for luck and went through to the front room.

It occurred to me that nothing I'd done so far had any obvious connection with the video girl. Evidence about her was scattered all over the room. I put my bundle down and took a closer look at the videos. Among the pre-recorded cassettes, European, British, American and Australian, were a lot of tapes for home recording. The names of movies presumably taped from TV were printed on the boxes—*The Left Hand of God, Marked Woman, The Running Man*—none of my favourites. I'd seen *The Running Man* way back, at a drive-in with my soon-to-be wife (later to be my ex-wife), Cyn. I saw it again on TV by accident. In it Laurence Harvey does the worst Australian accent in the history of the cinema. I couldn't understand why anyone

13

would want to tape it. For the hell of it, maybe to get a laugh at the accent, I put the cassette into the recorder and hit Play. It was worse than I'd thought—a long, boring sequence with some people seen on a boat at a distance. Barely focused. Arty. I hit Stop and picked up my bundle.

I was tired of the place, depressed by it and wanted to leave, but something was nagging at me, holding me back. I looked around noticing nothing new. Then the telephone rang, or rather emitted some of those electronic beaps that make you think you're out there with Spock on the *Enterprise*. I lifted the receiver and waited.

'Who's there?' a voice said—female, not young.

That's what I should be saying, I thought, but I said nothing.

'Who are you?' the voice said.

Hard to come up with an answer to that. What would someone good and comforting say? What would Phillip Adams say?

'Are you crazy? Lifting the blind and turning on the light in there? Do you want to be killed too?'

'You're talking about Carmel Wise,' I said, trying to sound like Phillip Adams.

'Yes. Don't you know they're watching the place most of the time? They're probably watching it now?'

'Who's they, Madam?'

'Who . . .?'

Press a bit harder, Cliff. 'I work for the owner of the Greenwich Apartments, Madam. Would you mind telling me who you are.'

'I don't want to get involved.'

You are involved, I thought. That's what everyone always says and it's true. Doesn't do to say so, though. Back to Phillip Adams. 'Please tell me . . .'

'No, nothing! Just be careful!' She slammed the

14

phone down so hard I winced and pulled the receiver from my ear. Then I dropped the envelopes and other things. I realised that I was standing opposite the window, in the middle of a frame like a TV news reader. I dropped to my knees and gathered up the papers. Then it seemed like a good idea to stay down there while I thought of a next move. Through the door, gun up, eyes blazing? The problem with that was I didn't have a gun with me. It made more sense to crawl across the floor to the window, knocking aside video cassettes as I went, and to sneak a look out into the courtyard.

Nothing had changed out there. Could be gun-men in the adjacent buildings, could be someone small crouched down behind the pedestal with an Uzi. I didn't think so. What I *did* know was that there was someone around who knew the telephone number of flat one and was concerned enough to ring it when she saw a light. From how many windows could that be done? That sort of inquiry would have to wait. The job now was to get home with my goodies.

I turned off the lights, pulled down the broken blind and opened the door. No-one lurking in the lobby. I patted my pocket. Yep, still got the key. Out into the courtyard, out into a cool night with the leaves of the plane trees rustling in a light breeze. Traffic noise from a distance and music somewhat closer. No shots, loud or silenced. I started across the courtyard to the lane and jumped a foot in the air as there was a rushing sound behind me. I almost dropped the envelopes again but it was just a jogger—a tall, thin jogger with headband, singlet and shorts and light, slapping feet.

'Hi,' he said. 'Sorry to startle you.' For an awful moment I thought he was going to be one of those who jog on the spot while they talk to you. Mustn't lose the aerobic effect whatever you do. But he just lifted

15

his hand and loped off down the lane.

I said, 'That's okay, have a nice run,' and followed him unaerobically. I stopped at the wine bar in Bayswater Road and had a drink. I had no trouble getting a place at the bar—the place must have been number three on the 'spots to be seen at' list.

3

NEXT morning I watched Helen while she made the coffee. She wore a red kimono-style dressing gown and looked terrific. She didn't feel terrific though—I could tell from the emphasis she gave to her movements. The cups hit the bench like sharp left jabs.

'You don't want me here, Cliff,' she said.

'You're wrong. I do want you.'

The percolator hissed and she went to the fridge for milk. 'Didn't feel like it last night. You hardly spoke and that was a perfunctory fuck.'

'I'm sorry.'

'Don't be sorry. Explain to me.'

'Explain what?'

She filled the cups and we sat down side by side at the bench. I put my arm around her and she let it stay there. She liked physical contact at the worst of times, so do I. It doesn't deflect her from her purpose though. 'When I come down from the bush to start the six months with you it's fine at first. Lovely for the first day, terrific for the next couple of days. You know why?'

I sipped. 'Tell me.'

'You're on holiday. When you go back to work it all changes. You close down. You go somewhere else. I get the fag-end of you.' She lit a Gitane. She smoked one a day, sometimes after lunch, sometimes after dinner; rarely first thing in the morning.

'It's difficult,' I said. 'The work's so shitty in some ways. Other parts of it I like more than anything else I've ever done.'

'Mm.' She smoked and drank coffee. 'I know all about men liking what they do.' Helen's husband, Michael Broadway, ran a vineyard and farm up on the north coast. According to Helen, he worked all through the daylight hours and fixed machinery and did laboratory tests at night. Seven days a week. They had a twelve-year-old daughter and a two-year-old arrangement—Helen spent six months on the farm and six months with me.

'I must meet up with Michael,' I said. 'We seem to be getting more alike all the time. Maybe that's a function of the arrangement. We should do an article for *Forum*.'

She touched my hand and I could feel her wedding ring. 'Don't get bitter, Cliff. We're talking, okay?'

'Okay.'

'Tell me about what you're doing.'

'Yes, Well, maybe you'll see what I mean. This girl got shot a week or so ago. I'm looking into it for her father. There's all kinds of strange angles.'

'Shot?'

'Shot dead. See? It's hard to come home and be . . . normal with that in the background. I have to think about it and . . .'

'I understand. Well, I've been thinking about it since you rolled off last night.'

'Come on, Helen . . .'

'It's all right. I'm going to get a place of my own.'

'Jesus!'

'Don't carry on. In this street if I can. Close by, anyway. I'll butt right into whatever you're doing and it can go to bloody hell if need be. I'll have that right. Otherwise you can be with me when you want to be and need to be. It'll be better. Not domestic. You'll like it.'

Like it? I thought. Like another failed relationship? But maybe she was right. 'You're incredible.' I kissed her and she turned her face and kissed me

18

back, hard. She smelled of coffee and tobacco and what two things ever went together better than those?

'I love Sydney and I love you. I'll have both. It'll work.'

I nodded. She was the finest diagnostician of human relationships I'd ever met. If she wanted it to work it probably would. She rinsed her cup and picked up the morning paper from the pile where I'd thrown it.

'I'll start looking today.'

'Can I help?'

'Nope.'

'Okay. How far back do those papers go?'

She riffled through the pile. 'Two weeks at least. Slob.'

She went off to shower and I dug through the papers for the reports on the shooting of Carmel Wise.

It had happened on a Friday night; I get two papers on Saturday morning so I had two accounts, two sets of photographs. The *National Herald*'s reporter fancied herself as a stylist: 'At 9 p.m. last night the courtyard outside the Greenwich Apartments was an oasis of quiet in a sea of sound. Kings Cross was at full blast all around, but in the leafy courtyard there *could* have been someone sitting down to read T. S. Eliot. They have a New York feel, the Greenwich Apartments, as if Woody Allen might wander through with his clarinet or Ivan Lendl might come bounding along on one of his late night runs. Instead, attractive Carmel Wise, 21, hot-shot videotape editor and movie buff, stepped out of Greenwich into hell . . .'

Helen came into the room dressed in white and smelling good. I couldn't see how any real estate agent could resist her. She'd probably get a penthouse with a view of the bridge and the choicest bits

19

of Darling Harbour. I was rumpled and unshaven. She looked over my shoulder.

'That's the one?'

'Yeah.'

'The story ran for a while. What was she called . . .?'

'The Video Girl. Helen, could you take a look at some woman's stuff. Give me your analysis?'

'You're not just trying to make me feel useful?'

'No.'

'All right.'

I cleared a space on the bench and spread out Tania Hester Bourke's belongings. Helen moved them around, looked at the photographs. She examined the purses, the sunglasses, the makeup and other items. I showed her the photo of Tania, glass in hand, smiling at the lens.

'What d'you want to know?'

'Anything you can tell me.'

'Mm, well. The passport is five years old, that's obvious, and the photographs,' she tapped the quarto-sized glossy black and white picture, 'is a couple of years later.'

'How can you tell?'

'Hair. Clothes.'

'There's two suitcases full of her clothes. Would you be able to tell how long ago they were bought? How long since they were worn?'

'Yes.'

'Great. Anything else?'

'She was an air hostess when the passport photo was taken.' She flipped through the passport. 'She went all over the place. By the time the other picture was taken she was doing something different. Look, she makes a few trips here and there in '82 and '83. Nothing like before. Same places—Singapore, Bangkok, Jakarta, but less often. I bet she's got batik cloth and a lot of silk stuff in the cases.'

20

'Right. What does that mean?'

'Nothing much. She's got expensive tastes to judge by the makeup. Ah ... you want to play Watson?'

'Sure.' I stroked an imaginary moustache.

'City girl, private school, no skills to speak of ... smoker, dieter ...'

'Come on.'

'She's a good bit thinner in the second photo. Did I ever tell you about when I put on a stone and half?'

'No.'

'I will one day. Point is, I know about dieting and the look it leaves. This woman's got it.' She poked at the documents. 'Fair bit of money passing through the accounts.' She ran a finger down a bank statement. 'But it's hard to tell with these things. It always looks like a lot, doesn't it?'

'Yeah, and it feels like nothing at all.'

Helen tapped the photos into a neat stack and put them aside. 'Well, that's all I can tell you for now. Um ... I've got enough for a deposit on something small. Wish me luck. I'm off.'

'Good luck.'

We kissed. We pressed together hard and thoughts of gunned-down girls and ex-air hostesses went out the window. She broke away and glanced at the photographs again. 'Oh, one more thing. Your mystery woman likes men.'

'Meaning?'

'She's not a lesbian. This is man-attracting equipment.' She dangled one of the gold sandals from her little finger. Helen's fingernails were short and painted a pale pink. She wore a couple of light silver bangles around her wrist that looked good against her tanned skin. 'And look at the picture—she fancies the bloke next to her.'

She was right. Tania had her hand on the arm of a big, blonde man. She looked as if she's just turned

21

her big brown eyes away from him for the sake of the photograph and that they'd be back on him soon.

'Husband?' I said.

She shook her head. 'No rings, not that that means much. No, I wouldn't say so. He doesn't look like the husband type.'

'There's a type?'

'Of course. Women can spot husbands, attached men, semidetached and so on, when they walk into a room. Usually, as soon as they open their mouths they confirm the guess. She won't be too hard to find, will she? You've got a ton of evidence.'

'Maybe not.'

'How does she connect to the girl who was shot?'

'I don't know. She lived in the flat the girl was using.' It struck me then that the suitcases could have come from somewhere else. 'Maybe she lived there.'

'Did they know each other?'

'I don't know.'

'Who took the photos?'

'I don't know that either. A man.' I pointed to the stuff that had belonged to Mr Greenwich. 'Are you serious?'

'What about? Getting my own place?'

The words sounded harsh and reproachful to me. I wanted to argue and convince her that she should stay right there. But I knew I'd be running all over the city that day and not be home until God knows when. I didn't have an argument to use. Helen knew it too. She looked determined but not reproachful. I drew a breath and scratched my stubble. 'No, I know you're serious about that. I mean about this attached and detached man business.'

'Yes.'

'Which am I?'

She slung her brown leather bag over her white linen shoulder and grinned at me. 'That's one of the things we'll find out, won't we?'

4

BACK to the papers. The *Herald* reporter had over-used her poetic licence. Further reading showed that Carmel Wise had not stepped *directly* into anything. She must have walked across the courtyard, 30 feet or so, before the bullets were fired. The damage to the sign suggested the direction from which the shots had come—from the left as you faced the Greenwich Apartments. The girl had been hit several times in the back and once in the head; I assumed the shooter was at ground level because any marked angle to the line of fire would have pinpointed a window. I was already starting to think of it as a professional job.

The *News* printed a photograph of the girl. She had a strong, high-cheekboned face with big eyes and a curious set of teeth, slightly gapped all around. The effect was pleasing. Her hair was dark and drawn back, giving her an intelligent, slightly surprised expression. She looked older than 21 and like someone who would be worth talking to.

The *News'* coverage was less lurid. Carmel Wise was dead when she was discovered in the courtyard by Mr Craig Wilenski, a resident of the block of flats opposite the Greenwich. This happened at 9.30 p.m. and there was no evidence for the *Herald's* nomination of 9 p.m. as the time of the shooting. Mr Wilenski was returning home at the time; he phoned from his own flat and was not a witness to anything. Neither was anybody else; no-one heard the shots, no-one heard anything suspicious.

But the man from the *News* must have filed what he had as quickly as he could and then pressed on because the Sunday edition carried the first of the 'Video Girl' stories. 'Police confirmed that the flat which Ms Wise had occupied contained hundreds of videotapes,' the story ran. 'The victim was carrying a bag in which there were more videotapes.' Then came the kicker: 'Videotapes were found in the pockets of the coat Ms Wise was wearing and in her Honda Civic sedan, parked several blocks from the courtyard in which she met her death.' She was 'the Video Girl' from that moment on.

The tabloids were in full swing by mid-week. The newshounds had learned that Carmel Wise had worked for all five Sydney television stations ('Video Girl Channel-hopped'), that she had appeared on quiz programmes as a movie expert ('Video Girl Knew 5000 Movie Plots') and that she had written, directed and produced a film for $10 000 which had made a bundle ('Big Bucks for Video Girl's Mini Budget Movie'). Personal details were very sparse—daughter of wealthy Sydney business man Leo Wise, educated at a Jewish private school, attended the National Film & Television School briefly. She had just completed work on a TV documentary on the ten richest people in Sydney, the producer of which, Tim Edwards, described her as 'a major talent with a great flair, perhaps too much flair for this project.'

By Thursday Carmel Wise was inside-page news at best. The police were calling for help from the public but the public wasn't helping. No-one had seen anything. The scribblers had looked up all the TV stars and 'personalities' who might have had any contact with Carmel Wise but had drawn blanks. A TV doctor who had known her slightly said that she was 'a very private person'. This got a small notice. Two nurses were killed on the North Shore and the 'Video Girl' slipped from sight. I saw no thing of the pornographic implications that Leo Wise had complained of, but they could have been exploited in other papers.

I made some more coffee and thought about it. Unlike most cases where there are only winks and nods to go on and the cops and journalists have muddied the waters, I had solid leads. I had Tania Bourke and Mr Greenwich and if the woman who'd called the flat the other night hadn't been a witness to the shooting I was a Frenchman. (I think we should stop knocking Dutchmen, *they're* not nuking Pacific islands and blowing up boats on our doorstep.)

I had almost too many leads. The question was whether to start with Tania Bourke and the man, or the witness, or get the official view on the case first. *Let your fingers do the walking*, I thought. I dialled the number for Frank Parker who had recently been elevated to Detective Inspector. While the phone was ringing I recalled that Frank had taken Hilde and their baby daughter away to Europe. Frank's first leave in years. His assistant, Barry Mercer, answered.

'Homicide.'

'You make it sound highly desirable, Mercer.'

'Who's this?'

'Hardy.'

'Frank's away.'

'I know, they've gone to show their baby London and Munich, their roots. I wonder what the baby'll make of it?'

'Well?' Mercer has no sense of humour, no babies either so far as I know. He's a thin, dark, intense young man who tries to think and feel the way Parker does. He has at least one problem there-Parker likes me and Mercer doesn't.

'I need some information on the Carmel Wise shooting.'

26

'Why?'

'The father's not happy.'

'Why?'

'Jesus, don't you ever say anything else?'

'Why isn't the father happy?'

I didn't want to tell Mercer about the mystery of flat one, not yet. 'The porno angle,' I improvised. 'He doesn't like it. Thinks you're on the wrong track.'

'That's solid,' Mercer said. 'Rock solid.'

I was surprised. 'I didn't read about it. There was nothing in the papers I saw.'

'There was a bit in the *Globe*. One of those snoopy bastards got onto it before we could stop him.'

'Stop him? Why?'

'I haven't got time to discuss it with you, Hardy. I'm up to my ears in work. We got another nurse this morning.'

'That's bad. Who's handling Wise?'

'Bill Drew, he's here. You want a word?'

'Yeah, thanks, put him on.'

'Before you go, how'd you know Frank and Hilde were . . . you know, showing the kid the cities?'

'Postcard. Didn't you get one?'

'No.'

'I'll put in a good word for you.'

'Fuck you. Here's Drew.'

I didn't know Drew so it was just as well he had a formal manner.

'Detective Constable Drew.'

'This is Cliff Hardy, Mr Drew. I assume Mercer's okayed it for you to fill me in a bit on the Wise matter.'

'I'll do what I can.' Cool, very cool.

'Professional job, would you say?'

'Certainly.'

'Mercer says you like the porno angle.'

'Looks like it. The movies in the shops are fairy-

27

floss—the real stuff circulates in the dark. Big money. We think the girl was involved, probably at the production end. She must have offended someone.'

'Why're you keeping this line of inquiry quiet?'

'Why d'you think?' he said impatiently. 'Look, we've got people out there, informers, people who hear things. But we'll get bugger all if those sleazos know we're interested.'

'Yeah. Well, her father says there were no dirty movies in the flat. I took a peep myself last night. All looked straight to me.'

There was a pause and the office noises became muffled. Drew must have put his hand across the mouthpiece. 'Just checking with Mercer,' he said. 'The stuff in the flat and the car were all right, but you should see what was in her bag.'

'Bad?'

'How long ago was it she was killed? A week and a half?'

'About that.'

'I saw some of this stuff that night. I haven't been able to fuck since. My wife's complaining. I'm thinking of applying for compensation.'

5

I showered, shaved and dressed. I don't know why but I didn't believe it. Perhaps it was the comments about Carmel Wise's flair as a filmmaker: I never knew a porno movie to have flair and as for artistic cutting, forget it. The ones I'd seen were mainly interesting from athletic and arithmetic points of view. I kept expecting someone to run on with a tape-measure but no-one ever did.

Leo Wise's conviction had something to do with it as well. He struck me as a shrewd man who'd assess his daughter as accurately as he would any-one else.

We'd left things the day before with an under-standing that I'd look at the flat, make some pre-liminary investigations and see if I thought there was anything he could gain from hiring me. Well, if the police were on the wrong track, there was. I decided that I was interested and I needed to know more about Ms Wise and the Greenwich Apart-ments and that I needed more of that shrewd as-sessment. I rang the number listed for Leo Wise In-vestments Ltd and made an appointment for 11 a.m.

That would take me into the city where I could check with Air Pacific on Tania Bourke. Another call got me a 1 p.m. appointment with the Personnel Manager of the airline.

All I needed to round things off was some line of attack on Mr Anonymous. I looked through his stuff and the photographs again, sifting carefully.

The notebook was battered and creased as if it had been carried around a lot and jammed into pockets it didn't really fit. The writing was large, squarish and upright. A military man? Bullshit! About 30 pages were written on—no names or addresses, just letters and numbers: Q 104; A 23; K 367; P 245: H 45; T 381 and so on. There was no pattern to it: some pages just had a number like Q 455 at the head followed by C 34, others had more entries—K 478; P 34; M 16; B 780; F 12; L 78; D 56 . . .

If there were such a thing as private detective school and if I'd been to it, I might have learned something about code cracking. As it was, I knew nothing about such things. I can't even do a cryptic crossword unless I train and practise at them for a month, building up slowly from the easy ones. I gave up on the notebook. I did find one thing I'd missed the night before. Tucked away in a crumpled tissue that had got into the stuff somehow was a piece of chalk. A school teacher? A billiards player? A pavement artist? I gave up on Mr Anonymous for the time being.

Leo Wise's office was in North Sydney. Smart man, there's a great view of the real city from North Sydney. I took the Glebe Island Bridge and followed the freeway up through Ultimo towards North Sydney. My Falcon likes freeways. In common with most old cars, it doesn't like to stop once it's got going; it doesn't even like to slow down too much. A few years ago, when we had a fuel crisis and everyone was driving around in fibreglass eggshells, the Falcon was a dinosaur, but not now.

It was a warm autumn day, almost cloudless with a light breeze. It hadn't rained for a while so the giant hole they're scraping alongside Darling Harbour, to be filled up with places that will act as suction pumps for money, wasn't a sea of mud the way it is in winter. From the freeway I could see the earth-moving machines creeping along on the scoured wasteland. Men in hard hats strolled around. Great to be in outdoors work on a day like this. Or in an air-conditioned car; I was sweating inside my cotton shirt and could feel my cotton trousers beginning to stick to the vinyl. I wound both windows down as I passed the patch of tall buildings Helen calls Little Manhattan. A breeze came up off the water as if it was specially for me and it cooled me down as I crossed the bridge.

I parked near the station and walked a couple of blocks to Napier Street. Wise's office was in one of those tall buildings that always seem to have good-looking women hurrying in and out of them. These places have pebbled areas in front of them with a few bushes struggling against the pollution, and a set of steps between the doors and the street which the women take without breaking stride. I'll follow one of them one day to see where she's going and why she needs the sunglasses on the top of her head.

The reception area of the building was like a brown-out zone in World War II. I groped my way to the noticeboard and practically had to put my nose up against it to discover that Wise Investments lived on the tenth level. The lift took the rest of my body up there quicker than my stomach. When I was reassembled I pushed open the glass door that was covered from top to bottom with the names of Wise's subsidiaries and associated companies. I wondered if he could recite them all without stumbling. A black woman with an American accent and French clothes told me that Mr Wise would see me now. A young man, groomed like a poodle and wearing a three-piece suit, led me through a vast open-plan office where about twenty people were sitting at desks picking up and replacing telephones. Their conversations appeared to be monosyllabic; they punched buttons on cal-

31

culators and smiled or grimaced according to the results. My escort knocked on a big door and pushed it open. His wristwatch beeped as he pushed.

'Thanks,' I said. 'Does that mean call Mother?'

He shook his head. 'New York calling in one minute.'

'Better hurry, mustn't keep New York waiting. They might sell you for dog food.'

I walked into the office. It was the size you'd need to play ping-pong in comfortably—two tables, of course. The carpet was thick and three of the windows were mostly glass. Two of them were covered with drapes, the other looked straight out down Lavender Bay. Wise was sitting behind a desk cluttered with files, computer printout sheets and newspapers. Above and behind him was a large painting of a beautiful dark woman with slightly gapped teeth. I looked at it as I made the trek to the desk.

'Moira,' Wise said. 'Second wife. Carmel's mother. Sit down, Hardy.'

I sat in a leather chair that felt good to sit in—right height, right back inclination. 'Any other kids, Mr Wise?'

'Two from my first marriage. Grown up and gone. Lance is in New York, I don't know what he does. Pauline drinks and gambles in . . . where is it, Nice? Monte Carlo? Somewhere like that.'

I nodded.

'Well, what've you got?' Wise said.

I told him about what I'd found in the flat and about the telephone call. He gave me his full attention, ignored the papers on the desk and the telephone when it rang sharply a couple of times but was picked up somewhere else.

'Tania Bourke,' I said. 'Air hostess at one time. The name mean anything to you?'

He shook his head. I told him about the police belief in the pornographic connection and about the

32

films in Carmel's bags. I edited out Drew's commentary.

'That's bullshit,' Wise said angrily. 'Carmel wasn't like that. The reverse, if anything.'

'I have to know a bit more about her, Mr Wise. What does that remark mean, for example? She wasn't interested in sex?'

He opened his hands like a card player showing he has nothing up his sleeves. His jacket hung on a stand by the door; his shirt cuffs were turned back and his tie was loose. He looked as if he'd worked hard at something every day of his life and was puzzled by people who didn't. 'That's what her mother told me. That's what it looked like.'

'No boyfriends?'

'A couple. Nothing serious. And no girlfriends either, if that's your next question. Shit, I wish there had been. I wish there had been something except films, films, and more bloody films . . .'

It sounds stagey but it wasn't. He was a distressed man not used to showing his distress. I suppose investment consultants don't as a rule. He clapped his hands to his head and ran them back over his hair. 'Something to do with that flat is behind this. I was sure of it before and I'm even more sure of it now. Clothes just left there, mystery photographs . . . That's your job. Find out what it was.'

'Okay, but it might not be as simple as that. Carmel might have known . . .'

'Look, Hardy. Let me try to make it clear to you. I believe my kid was a good kid who met with an accident. I want the murdering bastard who caused the accident to pay for what he did. I want that. But . . . an accident, you understand? I want my wife to be able to see it that way. Rule a line under it. Live with it and get on with living. Hell, she could have another kid. She's not old.'

Jesus, now I've got unborn life on my hands, I thought. The things a semi-pro is called on to do. 'Okay, Mr Wise. I hope it turns out the way you want. But I'll still have to know more about Carmel to do a proper job. Can I take a look at her place?'

'Sure. Get the address from the front desk outside. I forget the exact flat number. She shared with another girl. I'll have someone ring and tell her you're coming.'

'Right. I need the name of the agent who handles the Greenwich rentals.'

'Bushell and Kotch, Newtown. I'll advise them too.'

I stood and we shook hands across his untidy desk. He hadn't once said he was a busy man although he obviously was. Leo Wise was all right in my book. I really *did* hope it turned out to be a sort of hit and run.

I drove back across the bridge, picked up the Cahill Expressway and parked in Woolloomooloo. I had some time to kill before the Air Pacific appointment and I spent it walking beside the water and up through the Domain. A big Japanese ship was tied up, taking on cargo. I wondered if Helen and I should go on a cruise. Make love with the motion of the boat, drink cold wine on deck at night, read Somerset Maugham, eat pawpaw in Suva . . . Then I thought of the Bermuda shorts and the cameras and the flowers around the neck. Running away wasn't going to help; Helen was getting a place of her own and I was going to have to give a little, think of her first sometimes and myself second. It was going to be painful but worth it. Maybe.

I skipped lunch which meant that I was showing up for my second appointment of the day fuelled by two cups of coffee and fresh air. How does he do it?

The Air Pacific office decor confirmed my feelings

about the cruise. They way to see the islands was from a sailing boat with two or three other like-minded people. The giant posters of 747's landing on coral beaches against backdrops of fire-walking and water-skiing failed to excite me.

Mr Percy was a well-brushed character in horn-rims and a short-sleeved shirt. He didn't look like a grounded pilot, more like a computer sales-man. I opened by showing him my operator's licence and my serious manner.

He looked at the folder and then at the bank of filing cabinets behind him. His desk was bare apart from a telephone. 'I'm afraid I can't discuss our personnel with you, Mr . . . ' he glanced down at the licence, 'Hardy.'

'She's not current. I'd say she left Air Pacific two or three years ago.'

'Well . . .'

'If anything comes of this would you prefer the papers to say Air Pacific hostess Tania Bourke, or former air hostess Tania Bourke?'

'What could come of it? What is it?'

I shrugged. 'Who knows? You're information-rich.' I gestured at the filing cabinets. 'I'm information-poor.' I put the licence folder away. 'That's why I'm here.'

He got up, walked over to the cabinets and laid his hand directly on the right drawer. Out it came, riffle, riffle, and he pulled up a file. Back to the chair and the desk. I sat back in my chair to let him read and feel his power.

'What do you want to know?'

'When did she leave Air Pacific?'

He ran his finger down a page. 'March 1983.'

'Did she jump or was she pushed?'

'I beg your pardon?'

'Tell me whether she resigned or was she sacked?'

'I can't tell you that.'

'Come on, Mr Percy. Let's play cards. You tell me whether and I won't ask you why.'

A small smile escaped his tight, thin mouth. 'I suppose your job is something like mine—weighing people up, judging their capabilities.'

'Something like that. Some of it's sitting around doing nothing.'

He didn't like that which suggested to me that that was what he did some of the time. 'Yes, well, Miss Bourke joined the airline in 1977 and she left in 1983.'

I wrote 1977 in my notebook just to show willing. 'She held what position?'

That took him off-guard. 'Senior cabin . . . cabin attendant.'

'She was demoted?'

'I didn't say that.'

'No. Well, resignation or dismissal?'

'Dismissal.'

'Why?'

'You said you wouldn't ask that.'

'I lied to you.'

He closed the file and pushed his chair back from the desk, 'I think we've finished.'

I watched him while he found the place for the file. 'Just a minute!' I said.

He held the file poised above the drawer. 'What?'

'You can give me her address. That can't be classified information, surely.'

'I suppose not.' He opened the folder and glanced at the top sheet. 'Flat one . . .'

'Greenwich Apartments, at the Cross.'

He closed the folder, rammed it into the drawer and slammed the drawer home. I stood and let the wrinkles find comfortable places in my shirt and pants. 'Don't worry, Mr Percy,' I said. 'You'll make it.'

'What d'you mean?'

'Percy of Personnel doesn't sound so good. Percy of Flight Operations sounds a lot better. You'll make it.'

'Good afternoon, Mr ... Hardy.'

6

CARMEL Wise's flat in Randwick was near the Prince of Wales Hospital in one of those streets that took their names from the Crimean War. That was a pretty safe war to take a name from—nobody remembers who won or lost what. I parked outside the block, set back from the road with a nice stand of silver birch trees in front of it, and wondered what I was going to run into next. Another video freak? A landscape gardener? A lesbian builder? The middle class was getting more complicated all the time.

The day had turned cool suddenly. Clouds across the sun and an edge to the breeze. I took my jacket off the back seat and shrugged into it while I waited to cross the street. I thought a contemplative walk in Centennial Park might be in order after this call. Something to sharpen the already sharp appetite and stimulate the powers of observation. I didn't expect much from this call. In this block of flats I had a name and a number. The next visit would be harder—to the flats flanking the Greenwich Apartments, where I had nothing to go on but the sound of a voice on the telephone.

I ducked across between a truck and a motor cycle and searched for a break in the silver birches. It took the form of a narrow brick path, artistically overgrown and lightly layered with dog shit. Small dog shit—there was nothing crude or obvious around here. I walked up the path, through smoked glass doors and up carpeted steps. No dog shit. Carmel

Wise's name was still on the tenants' board, under glass, bracketed with that of Judy Syme—Studio Eight, Stage Three. Studio? Stage? Of course.

I ignored the lift and took the stairs. What, pass up a chance to ascend by foot to Stage Three? Not Hardy. As I was bounding up, almost bouncing off the walls, I was aware of someone coming up behind me. A young man, long fair hair, jeans and T-shirt. An artist, no doubt. I got to Stage Three and knocked on the door of Studio Eight. Before I'd regained my breath, I felt his hand on my shoulder. He pulled and I came around with the pressure.

'What ...?' I said.

He punched me in the stomach, or tried to. There was some space between me and the door and I used it to shove my spine back as I saw the punch coming. That took some of the steam out of it but there was enough left to make it hurt in my slightly winded state. He was big, his biceps bulged in his T-shirt sleeves and there was no fat on him. But he was more used to standing or lying still and lifting things than to moving and hitting. He swung at me with his big right arm and I swayed away from it and hooked him in the ribs. Then he swung his big left arm, reasonable thing to do, but a bit obvious; I blocked it and spun him around so that he hit the door with his back stiff and his head thrown back. He hit hard and sagged. Then the door was pulled open and he pitched back. I stepped aside and watched him fall.

'Michael! What are you doing?' A woman with wet hair and wearing a white bathrobe stood in the doorway.

'He's looking for his contacts,' I said. Michael started to struggle up and I put my foot on his back and pushed down hard.

'Don't do that!' She shook her head and a spray of water covered me.

'Tell him not to assault people who knock on your door then.'

'Knock? It sounded like a horse hitting it.'

I lifted my foot and let Michael stand. He was red in the face and puffing. He flicked his fair hair back and brushed dirt off his T-shirt. Nothing looks sillier than a muscle man trying to think.

'I thought . . . I thought he was one of them,' he said.

'One of who?'

'Never mind,' she said. 'Who are you?' She took a step back and alarm showed in her face. Good face, as dark and intelligent as Michael's was fair and stupid. I took out my stamped and signed ID and showed it to her.

'Didn't Mr Wise's office phone to say I was coming?'

'Oh God, of course. Michael, you are an idiot!'

'Don't understand,' he muttered.

'He's here about Carmel.'

'So were they,' Michael said.

'Now *I* don't understand,' I said. 'Can we go in and have a talk?'

'Yes. Come on. I'm sorry.'

'Me too?' Michael said.

'Definitely,' I said. 'Hope I didn't hurt you.'

He looked glum and pushed past me following the woman. Studio Eight was a big room with a polished wood floor, white walls and huge windows. The trees of Centennial Park looked close enough to touch. There were posters on the walls, paintings and carvings. The cooking and eating went on at one end and there were two doors, evidently to bedrooms in the wall opposite the fireplace. Cushions and beanbags over by the windows, a big stereo, no television.

The woman pulled the sash of her robe tighter and held out her hand. 'Judy Syme.' She nodded at the man who'd thrown himself down on one of the big cushions. 'This is Michael Press.'

'Cliff Hardy.'

Press looked like a big, lazy dog lying on the cushion. 'Who is this guy, Jude?'

'You tell him. I'll put some clothes on. I was having a shower when you two started to batter my door down.'

I walked over to the window and looked out over the park. I could see a bit of the racecourse too, but I preferred the park which is free—the racecourse costs you money. 'Carmel's father hired me to investigate her death. He thinks the police are on the wrong track.'

'What track are they on?' Press rubbed his ribs where I'd hooked him. 'You a boxer ever?'

'Amateur only. They think she was a porno queen. A peddler of smut.'

Press laughed. The laugher started and he couldn't stop it even though it apparently hurt his ribs. He rolled on the cushion and slapped the floor. Judy Syme came out wearing a tracksuit and sneakers.

'What now?' she said. 'Stop it, Michael, you fool.'

Press gasped and stifled the mirth. 'He says the cops think Carmel was dealing in dirty movies.'

'Huh.' She took a packet of cigarettes from a slit pocket in the front of the suit and lit up. She was slim and nervous looking, too impatient to look pretty. 'That's nonsense. Nobody who knew Carmel could possibly think that. She regarded porn movies as . . .,' she waved the cigarette, '. . . nothing.'

'Did you tell the police that?'

'They wouldn't listen. They hardly asked.'

'D'you remember the name of the policeman you talked to?'

'No.'

'Drew?'

'Yes.'

41

'What did he do here?'

'Nothing much—looked in her room. There's nothing to see—some clothes and books. You can have a look too if you like.'

I nodded. 'Okay, in a minute. Tell me why Michael here got so heavy and who you mean by "they"?'

She dropped the cigarette into a dish on the ledge over the fireplace. It hissed and a curl of smoke floated up. 'Would you like a drink?'

'I would,' Press said.

'Michael drinks light beer. I drink wine. Which would you prefer?'

'Wine, thanks.'

'Eight per cent,' Press said.

'What?'

'Alcohol. That's too much.' He slapped his hard, flat stomach. 'It'll put the weight on.'

'I worry it off,' I said. Judy Syme came back with a can of Swan Light lager and two glasses of white wine. She lowered herself onto a cushion without spilling a drop. I crouched awkwardly, got my bum on the floor and let my legs move forward.

'You're stiff,' Press said. He popped his can and I accepted my glass. First nourishment since breakfast.

'Cheers,' I said. 'I may be stiff but I haven't got bruised ribs.'

'Stop it,' Judy Syme said. 'I wish Michael had been around in the time before Carmel got shot.'

'Why? What happened?'

She took a sip. 'Some men came here. Twice. Looking for Carmel.'

'What did they do?'

'Barged in, pushed me around. Trashed her room.'

'What did they say?'

'Nothing.'

'Twice you said. When was this?'

'The first time was a week or so before . . . before

she got killed. The second time was the night before.'

'Did you tell Drew this?'

She lit another cigarette. 'Yes. He took down the descriptions, but he didn't seem very interested.'

I got my notebook from my jacket pocket. 'Give me the descriptions.'

'One of them looked like you,' Press said.

'I thought you weren't here.'

'Judy told me about them. One was a thin, tall guy with a broken nose, hard-looking, like you.'

'Thanks. Anything else?'

They looked at each other the way people do when trying to recall a conversation. Who sat where, who said what? 'I don't think so,' Judy Syme said. 'Oh, of course, he was a New Zealander.'

'Who?'

'The one that looked like you.'

I wrote 'NZ' beside 'looks like self'. 'What about the other one?'

'Fatter,' Judy said. 'And fairer, less hair except he had a moustache. They wore suits. They looked like police but they weren't.'

'How do you know?'

'I'm a nurse, I've met a lot of police. I know.'

'I see. Well, what did Carmel say about this? Where was she?'

'She was working the day they came the first time. I told her that night and she took off. Packed a few things and took off. She didn't come back. The same two came back later, like I say.' She took a big drink of her wine and dragged on the cigarette. 'And the next day I read in the paper that she was dead.'

'Did these heavies ask you where she was?'

'Yeah. I wouldn't tell them.'

'Did they threaten you?'

She nodded. 'They hit me, but I wouldn't tell them. Fuck them, I thought.'

Press drained his can and looked admiringly at her. I took a drink and privately toasted her courage myself. 'Did Drew ask you where she'd gone?'

'He might have. I forget. I didn't tell him anyway. I got the feeling that he didn't care. What you say about the pornography explains it. What a laugh!'

'Will you tell me? I don't think she was involved in pornography either.'

'Sure I'll tell you. She was with Jan De Vries. He's a lecturer at the Film & Television School. They were working on something together.'

'What?'

'I don't know. Something that took all her time and energy. Something very important to her. We shared here for nearly two years. I was around when she was finishing *Bermagui*, but I never . . .'

'Sorry. Finishing what?'

'*Bermagui*, her first movie. You haven't seen it?'

'No.'

'It's brilliant.'

'Brilliant,' Press said.

Judy stood and got rid of her cigarette in the same way as before. 'This one would have been brilliant too. For sure. Christ, she worked at it. And now . . .' She wrapped her arms round her upper body and swayed. Press jumped up and took hold of her. She let him hug her. 'I miss her. She was terrific. So intense. She never wasted a single minute. Not like the rest of us, drinking and everything. She could work for three days and nights straight. Does that sound like a porno freak to you?'

I shook my head. I was the only one sitting down but her anger was so strong that I felt she should have the stage, have the space to say what she wanted to say. 'No,' I said quietly. 'I'm sure you're right about that. Her father feels the same way.'

She detached herself from Press and turned to look out the window. 'As fathers go he seems to be all right. Carmel loved him.'

'Did she love anyone else?'

She shook her head. 'No, I don't think so.'

I looked at my notebook. 'Jan De Vries?'

She grinned. 'Wife and two kids. She fucked him but I don't think she'd let a wife and two kids screw up her work.'

I pulled my legs up and got slowly to my feet. 'Thanks.'

'For the wine?'

I emptied the glass and put it on the ledge beside the dead butt dish. 'Come on, Judy. You don't have to be tough. You've lost your friend. I've lost a few in my time. It hurts.'

'So what does her father want? Revenge?'

'Partly, it's natural.'

'Right,' Michael Press said.

I told her about Leo Wise's wish to understand his daughter's death. To see it as an accident. I mentioned the possibility of another child.

'Oh, great!' she said.

'You don't understand. He's older than you, older than me. My grandmothers had about nine or ten kids each. Maybe five or six of them survived. Your great-grandmothers probably did the same. They expected some wastage. My father was the last in the bunch. Your grandfather might've been in the same spot. You mightn't be here if they hadn't operated that way back then. It was healthy in a way. Don't knock it.'

She went very still and looked at me. 'I never thought of it like that.'

'Can I have a look at her room, please?'

'Sure.' She walked over and opened the door nearest the window. I went into a big room with plenty of light. Better view of the racecourse from here. The room held the usual things—double bed, chest of drawers, built-in wardrobe, bookcase. A big TV set and a VCR were on a trolley at the foot of the bed. A door led to an *en suite* bathroom. I glanced

45

around but rooms give off an aura like people; I sensed that there was nothing to be learned here.

Judy Syme stood in the doorway smoking again. 'Go ahead. Look through her undies.'

'I don't think so.' I ran my eye along the bookshelf. Mostly titles to do with films, a few novels, a few left-wing political works. There was a cassette on top of the TV set and I picked it up. 'Bermagui' was hand-printed on a label stuck to the plastic case. 'Can I borrow this? Her film?'

She shrugged. 'Sure. I'd like it back. She gave it to me. It probably sounds sloppy but I was watching it in here the other day.'

'I understand. Did she ever keep cassettes here?'

'Oh, sure. She had them all here at first. But they just got to be too many. They were everywhere so she asked her father if she could use that flat in the Cross.'

'Did you ever go there?'

'Once. Creepy joint. This crazy old woman came to borrow sugar. Sugar!'

'What old woman?'

'From the flats across the courtyard. Weird old girl with purple hair. Carmel gave her some sugar.'

'Hmm. Where did she do her work? I mean editing and all that?'

'Various places. Studios. The equipment isn't exactly stuff you have around the house. Jan De Vries would know.'

We went back into the other room. Michael Press was flexing his muscles in front of his reflection in a window. He didn't seem to mind us catching him. I shook Judy Syme's hand and gave her one of my cards.

'Thanks for your help. Please call me if you can think of anything that might be useful.'

She held on to my hand a little longer than was

necessary, as if I formed some sort of connection with her friend. 'Okay,' she said.

I turned just before I opened the door. 'You don't have any clues on what those men wanted, do you? Or on why she was killed?'

'I haven't the faintest idea.'

7

IT was late afternoon, the tree shadows would be long in the park and I could sit by the lake and look at the ducks. On expenses, not bad. First I called Helen from a public phone.

'Hello,' she said. 'Where're you?'

'Randwick.'

'Really? That's where I might end up.'

'It didn't go too well, the flat-hunting?'

'Lousy.'

'I'm sorry. Look, I've got another call to make. I'll be home around six or so. We'll go out. Okay?'

'All right. Maybe.' She hung up. After that I didn't feel like the walk in the park anymore. I didn't feel like tramping up and down stairs questioning people about a murder either, but I had no choice.

I drove in to the Cross but ended up parked close to White City. Some of the courts were in the shade, some were still fully in the sun. *Be nice down there,* I thought. Forehand, backhand, lob, smash. I could see people on the courts doing just that—small white shapes darting about. Doing something just for fun; should be more of it. But then, there should be more of a lot of things—rain in Africa, B. B. King cassettes and small flats in Glebe Point, evidently.

I put *Bermagui* in the glove box and locked it. I locked the car too, took an envelope with a selection of the photographs, including the one of Tania Bourke, and walked. Away from the sporting scene,

48

business before leisure, past the temptation of the wine bar and up the lane to the Greenwich Apartments. A jogger swerved around me—a woman this time, with matching head and wrist bands. Nothing had changed in the courtyard; the arrangement of the flanking buildings allowed a fair bit of the late afternoon sun to penetrate. I sat on the empty pedestal and felt the warmth the bricks had retained. There were two apartment blocks to consider, maybe a dozen places with windows that permitted a view of the courtyard and activity in flat one of the Greenwich. I was there at the right time. It was odds on that the person I wanted was the weird old girl with purple hair. Do weird old girls go out to work? Not usually. I tucked my shirt firmly into my pants, pulled my collar straight and buttoned my jacket. Notebook and licence folder in hand, evidence in an envelope, the private detective goes to work. Bullshit. I went to the winebar and bought a packet of Sterling cigarettes and a bottle of Mateus Rosé. I was ready for the purple hair.

I drew six blanks in the building on the left. I tried every apartment with the right aspect: two no answers, two were occupied by young women who weren't interested once they found I wasn't there on business. The fifth resident was a middle-aged man who would have talked about anything from the price of gold to the Iran-Iraqui war. Loneliness wailed from the bare room behind him as he stood in the doorway. There was an old woman in the sixth flat; she had a raspy voice like the telephone caller, was about the right age and her windows were in the right place, but her hair was bright, buttercup yellow.

I found her on the second try in the other building. She was small and thin and her face was creased and rumpled like an old passionfruit. She could have been 80 or maybe she was just a 60-year-old who'd been busy. The purple hair was like a kindergarten kid's wild drawing; she had bright blue stuff around her eyes and her caved-in mouth was like a sunset—yellow teeth and bright red lips.

'Yes?' She teetered on high heels and had to hang on to the door for support. She'd already started, perhaps she never stopped.

'Good afternoon, Madam,' I said. 'I believe we talked on the telephone the other night.'

'What?' She had the door on a chain and was peering up at me through the four-inch gap. I showed her the licence.

'I have to get my glasses,' she said. She left the door on the chain and I slipped two fingers through and slid the catch free. The door was standing open and I was head and shoulders inside when she got back.

She laughed. 'I always do that. Someday someone'll come in and kill me.'

'You need a gun,' I said.

'I had one but I lost it. Well, you're in. Let me see that paper again.' She hooked on a pair of wire-rimmed glasses and squinted at the licence. 'Private Inquiry Agent,' she read. 'I knew one of them once. Way back in the forties. Drank himself to death. Funny thing, I drank just as much as he did an' I'm still here. Whaddayou think of that?'

'You must have a fine constitution,' I said. I held up the Rosé. 'Haven't retired, have you?'

'No fear. Come in. I have to warn you, I can drink all day an' all night an' it doesn't affect me.'

'You like to talk, don't you?' I went into the living room which was full of furniture that all looked too big for her. So did the room itself with its high ceiling, picture rail all around and deep, floral carpet. I went over to the window. 'Excuse me,' I said. I parted the dusty Venetian blinds and looked directly down from one storey into the courtyard.

The window of flat one in the Greenwich Apartments was directly opposite.

'Feel free,' she said. 'I'll get some glasses.'

I sat on the arm of an overstuffed sofa, reached across and put the bottle on the glass top of a French-polished table. She came back with two tall glasses—long stems, green tinge, swirling designs cut in the glass. She took the foil off the bottle expertly and poured carefully.

'Cheers,' she said. 'I'm Ellen Barton, Mr Hardy, and I'm very pleased to meet you.' She drank and hiccupped. 'Excuse me.'

I drank too. At least it was cold. 'That was a very dangerous thing you did, Mrs Barton, making that phone call.'

'Ellen,' she said. 'I thought I was anonymous. How did you find out it was me?'

I told her. She nodded and finished her wine. She let about half a minute pass before she poured some more. 'I remember that day. Gee, she was a nice kid.'

'So everyone says.'

'Yeah, a nice kid. So what's your interest?'

I told her. She listened but she seemed to have trouble concentrating. She twitched a little inside her blue silk dress with its beaded top and wide, unfashionable belt. The buzzing of a fly distracted her; she seemed to be watching motes in the beams of light that slanted through the blinds.

'Did you see the shooting, Ellen?'

'Sort of.'

'What do you mean?'

'Wouldn't have a smoke on you, would you?'

I produced the silver packet and she pounced on it greedily. 'Very nice too. You gonna have one?'

I shook my head. She lit up and puffed luxuriously. 'Remember de Reszke, in the tins?'

'No.'

51

'Ah, they were lovely cigarettes. Not like the rubbish they sell now. 'Course, these are all right.'

'The shooting,' I said.

'Yes, I saw it. That is, I was looking out the window and I heard the shots and I saw her fall.'

'You didn't see who did it?'

'Not properly. Look, why're those flats empty over there?'

I told her about Leo Wise's plans for the Greenwich Apartments. It was hard to keep her mind on a single subject; I couldn't tell whether the wine was making her that way or whether she'd be worse without it. She had nearly finished her second glass. 'Tell me what you saw?'

'A man. That's all. In the corner. He ran across and down the lane. He . . .'

'What?'

'He jumped over her. Jumped!'

'Would you recognise him again?'

She shook her head; the purple hair wobbled. 'Dark. Couldn't see properly. Bastard!'

'What did you do?'

'Nothing.'

'Why?'

She stubbed out the cigarette and poured some more wine. Her hand shook and she spilled some on the table. 'Bugger it. Know how long I've lived here?'

I shook my head.

'Forty years. Think I haven't seen it before? Shooting? I've seen it! You can't do anything.'

'You did something the other night. You rang the flat.'

'I'd had a few. I felt sorry for her.'

'How did you know I wasn't the killer?'

'You used a key. Looked like you had a right there. But, he *was* a tall man, same as you. I like a big man.'

52

'Mm, well, what happened then?'

'After a bit, ambulance came up the lane. Police. I put out the lights and went to bed. Didn't sleep much, but.'

'Did the police interview you?'

'Yeah. One came. Told him I was asleep. Didn't hear or see anything. Look, three, no four people been shot around here. Police never caught one killer. Not one. Have some more plonk, sorry rosey. 's good.' She wasn't the drinker she thought she was, two and a bit glasses, admittedly big ones, and she was awash. Of course, I didn't know what sort of a foundation she was building on. She lit another cigarette, just managing to get the match in the right place. Forty years, she'd said. I wondered if she could unscramble them.

'Before the girl ...' I began.

'Remember Jack Davey?' she said suddenly.

I *did* remember him. He was the best thing on radio in the days before transistors, the Top Forty, and talk-back. 'Sure,' I said. 'Hi ho, everybody.'

''s right! 's right! Hi ho, every ... everybody. Ooh, he was a lovely man, Jack Davey.'

'I don't see ...'

'Jack Davey had a girlfriend who lived in that flat.'

She leaned forward conspiratorially as if the gossip was still hot stuff although Jack Davey has been dead for nearly 30 years. 'Lovely girl, showgirl or something. He used to come and visit her. Silver hair, beautifully brushed always. And he wore a camel-hair coat. Funny thing, that ... people wore coats more. Must've been colder. Must be the bomb ...'

She was back in the forties, with her dipso private eye and Jack Davey, and I wanted her in the eighties as neighbour to Tania Bourke and Mr Anonymous. The problem was to get her there. 'Did anyone else famous live there, Ellen? In the Greenwich?'

'Oh, sure. 'Course, I forget their names. Been a long time. Lee Gordon, he was there, or a friend of him. Anyway, they held parties there. Parties! You shoulda seen them! Packed! You couldn't squeeze another bottle in.'

She laughed at her joke and took another drink. Gordon was an entrepreneur who'd brought the big names out from America, Sinatra and the rest, and made a bundle by putting them on in the Stadium. Gordon died and the Stadium was pulled down, but this was better—sixties. 'Do you remember a man and a woman who lived there, I'd say about two or three years back.'

'Too long ago.'

'Come on, you remember Jack Davey.'

'Jack Davey . . . lovely silver hair, all brushed.'

I took out the photograph of the group around the table. 'Look at this. Do you know her?'

She reached for the glasses and put them on. A sip and a puff and she was ready. 'Ooh, yes. I remember her. Air hostess.'

'That's right. Do you remember the man?'

'Yes, yes. See him alla time.'

'What? You see the man who lived in the flat? You see him now?'

'No, no, no.' She slapped my arm. 'Silly. No, haven't seen him for years. I mean this one.' She put her finger next to the face of the blonde man, the one Tania Bourke was giving the big Yes to.

'Who is he?'

'Darcy. Heard one'a the girls call him Darcy. Runs one of the clubs down th' road. Probably other places too . . . money, y'see. Still lives there—flat over th' club. Right? Inna old days they all usta live inna city, th' people with th' money. Jack Davey. Now where d' they live? Inna country. Look at that John Laws. Farmer! Talks about th' farm onna
54

radio all th' time. That's no way for a pers'nality t'be. Jack Davey wouldna known one end of a cow from another.'

'He was the same with horses, I understand,' I said. 'Which club, Ellen?'

'Champagne Cabaret. Down the road. Not surprised he knew her. She was a pretty girl.'

'Did you know them? Talk to them?'

She shook her head. The cigarette was between her lips and ash flew. 'Naw. They weren't there much.'

'You remember the man?'

'Bit.'

'What did he look like?'

'Ordinary. Wore a uniform.'

'What kind of uniform? Pilot's uniform?'

'No. Don't think so. No wings 'n that.'

'Police?'

More head-shaking, more ash. 'Like police but different. Blue. I don't know. Johnny O'Keefe went to Lee Gordon's parties . . .'

She was tired and drunk, ready to slip back among her souvenirs. I swallowed the rest of my wine and she did the same. The bulb-shaped bottle was almost empty. She poured some more wine and ran her fingers over the surface.

'That's pretty. I'll put flowers in it. Flowers remind me of funerals, but. That poor kid. I've seen a lotta funerals.'

I stood and took a few steps towards the door. She got to her feet slowly and came across the carpet putting her feet down on the red roses on the carpet, avoiding some purple splotches. 'Usta be a dancer,' she said. 'C'n tell, can't you? Never lose it. That kid, she moved nice too. I remember how she moved, real light an' nice. An' then he shot her . . .' She ran her sleeve over her eyes and spread the blue makeup across her forehead.

I put a card on a table by the door. 'Ring me if you

55

think of anything. Wait a minute. You said she moved lightly, like a dancer?'

''s right.'

'What about the bag? It must have been heavy.'

'Bag? What bag? She didn't have a bag.'

8

I drove past the Champagne Cabaret on the way home but I didn't stop. You don't go into those sorts of places at six in the evening looking for the boss. You go in at midnight and you make sure you're sober because the odds are nobody else around will be, and that gives you an edge. You take a gun with you too, if you have one, and some back-up, also sober if possible.

I got home about an hour after I said I would. Helen was sitting in a chair reading *Democracy* by Joan Didion and drinking whisky by Johnny Walker.

'Hi,' she said. She held up her glass. 'Join me?'

I stood behind her chair and looked at the book. It was creased and battered as if it had been in and out of her bag or pocket many times. I judged that she'd put in a day of sitting around and waiting. I touched the top of her head, smoothed down her hair. 'No, think I'll have some wine.'

'Ah, you're going out again later.'

'I'm supposed to be the detective.' I went through to the kitchen and got the drink. I still had the cassette and the envelope in my hand. Helen pointed.

'Are we watching a movie tonight?'

'This was made by the girl who got killed. I want to see it. Tell me about the flat-hunting.' I sat down opposite her and pulled the chair closer so that our knees touched.

'Crummy dumps,' she said. 'One good one but it costs the earth.'

57

'D'you have to do it?'

'Of course I do. Look, you're going to watch a dead woman's film and then go out to get yourself beaten up or have some depressing conversation. What am I supposed to do?'

I drank some wine and didn't speak.

'You hardly worked at all the last time I was here.'

'That's the way it happens sometimes.'

'How long will this job last?'

I shrugged. 'A week. A month.'

Helen drank some whisky. She sighed, looked at her book and then threw it on the floor. 'I just don't want to be a pain,' she said. We reached out for each other and hugged awkardly, sitting in our separate chairs. We held the hug for quite a while until it turned into something else which we finished off in bed.

I made sandwiches and took them and some wine upstairs and we ate in bed. Helen told me about the fifteen real estate agents she'd visited and the dozen or so houses and flats. Then she fell asleep.

It was after nine but still way too early to go to the Champagne Cabaret. I made coffee and put the cassette in the VCR.

The screen filled with an expanse of water; still, silver water that was suddenly broken by the leaping, cavorting bodies of what looked like thousands of dolphins. They jumped and flapped and the sound of their squeaking, barking calls filled the room. I turned the sound down. The word 'Bermagui' came up in deep blue over the fractured silver of the dolphins at play, and some music, mostly strings and drums, accompanied the credits. The film was written, edited, produced and directed by Carmel Wise.

I'm no movie buff; I'd see about six or seven new films a year and catch another dozen or so on TV and video. I like them fast and funny—Woody Allen, anything with Jack Nicholson, that sort of thing. Carmel Wise's picture was nothing like Woody Allen, and her hero, a thin, toothy character, was more like Donald Sutherland than Nicholson. But it was a marvellous film. I forgot I was watching for professional reasons: the simple story of a schoolteacher in love with one of his students against the background of a quiet town, caught in the annual tourist rush and under pressure from the moneyed people of Canberra who were buying up the beach, grabbed me and swept me along.

The acting was fine—underplayed, done without the usual clangers and dead lines that disfigure films made by inexperienced people. The supporting cast were virtually silent which was another plus; they rapped out dramatic interjections while the main players wove the story. Most of all, the filming was terrific: Carmel Wise had resisted the clichéd shots and had got the hard ones—the old house, crumbling and wisteria-covered, but still looking strong and appropriate; the beach party, slowly getting out of hand as the booze flummoxed and confused the kids, turning them from sharp and funny to slow and dull.

The 90 minutes passed quickly. I felt like applauding when the film finished and I ran the tape back to watch bits again to make sure I hadn't imagined it. But it was all there—the sure touch, the wit in the use of the camera, the low-key emotion and the economy of the whole thing. As the final credits rolled again—brief, with a lot of the same people doubling up on the jobs, I reflected that Carmel Wise was a real loss to the city, to the nation. I was also sure that she wouldn't have been interested in pornography. What else? I tried to grab the impressions quickly: strong social conscience, political radical with a sense of humour, more humanist than feminist, scourge of the rich ... the name Jan de Vries came up on the screen— 'thanks to Jan de Vries for criticism and coffee'.

After eleven, time to go. I got my Smith & Wesson.38 Police Special from the kitchen drawer and checked it for load and action. A quick wash, a fresh shirt, holster harness on, gun away and I was ready. Images from the film floated in my mind as I drove through the quiet streets. A long shot of the beach at night, two cigarettes glowing in the dark, occupied me along Glebe Point Road and I thought about the love-making between the teacher and the student as I drove up William Street. Then I thought about Helen in my bed and her flat and other beds. As I looked for a parking place I wrenched my mind back to the job. It shouldn't be too hard. Chat to one nightclub owner about some old pals. He'd probably be only too pleased to help, probably give me a free drink and introduce me to some nice girls.

The streetwalkers were at their posts on Darlinghurst Road, behaving themselves as the cops walked past, and then laughing and giving their blue-shirted backs the finger. The eating and drinking and game-playing places were open and doing business. The Champagne Cabaret was a few doors from Woolworths which was closed. There were people squatting in the long, deep recess in front of the store—some jewellery sellers, a pavement artist and a man just standing there, doing nothing.

The man outside the joint was working hard. 'Come on gents,' he called, 'come on ladies, come on all you folks in between. Something for everyone at the Champagne Cabaret. They sing, they dance, they make romance. Come in, sir. Hey, sailor!' He was about 21 in the body and twice that in the face. He wore a draped jacket with shoulder pads and

60

skin-tight pants, something like the outfit I used to wear myself in Maroubra around 1956. I stopped to look at the photographs mounted in glass cases beside the narrow doorway. Sequinned women clutched microphones suggestively; too-sleek men clutched sequinned women.

He waved his cigarette in my face. 'Come right in, sir. Ten dollars an' you're through the door an' in another world. You look like a good sport. Do yourself a good turn.'

'I want to talk to the boss,' I said. 'Big blonde guy, isn't he? Darcy, is that right?'

He kept waving the cigarette and spoke to the passers-by. 'Come right in, ten dollars to make your dreams come true.'

'No trouble,' I said. 'Just a talk.'

He looked directly at me for a split second. 'Twenty dollars to make your dreams come true.'

'You said ten before.'

'That was then, this is now.'

'I could walk right through you.'

'Into a locked door,' he said. 'Come on, gents, come on, girls . . .'

I gave him the twenty and he almost made a bow. 'Pay at the door,' he said.

Past the photographs, with my foot on the first step, I spun around. 'What?'

'Pay at the door, arsehole. Ten dollars to make your dreams come true.'

Smoke and noise drifted towards me as I went down the stairs. There was hardly room to stand between the bottom stair and the door and a man was already standing there. I gave him ten dollars and he pushed the door open. The Champagne Cabaret had taken its decor ideas from a variety of sources; there were Arabian and Chinese touches in the lighting and the wall paintings, a Broadway effect to the stage which was decorated in black and

61

white like a piano keyboard and even a Hollywood western look to the bar and tables. I saw this through the smoky gloom as I pushed towards the bar. Pushed, because the joint was full; people were dancing on a small floor in the middle of the room, spilling over into the area occupied by tables and even putting the people standing at the bar under pressure.

I eased out of the way of a tightly embraced couple and managed to get to the bar. The music, which had been a sort of pseudo-Glenn Miller swing, petered out. The dancing stopped; a drum rolled and a man in a white dinner jacket came out onto the stage.

'Ladies and gentlemen, the Champagne Cabaret is delighted to present—Ricky Gay!'

A tall person with cleavage and curves and a blonde wig wriggled onto the stage, adjusted a silver lamé shoulder-strap and began to sing 'Big Spender'. About half the people were interested in the singer, the other half were interested in each other and the booze. Three topless waitresses and the drinkers at the bar kept two barmen in red waistcoats busy. The place was hot and the barmen were sweating; I waited until I caught one of them taking a break to mop his face.

'I'd like to see Mr Darcy,' I said. 'Is he here?'

'I serve drinks,' he said.

'Then I'll take a Scotch and ice and could you tell me where to find Darcy?'

He put away the handkerchief and made the drink. His hands were fast and if they were sweaty it didn't seem to inconvenience him. He put the drink in front of me. His red face glowed under the light coming from behind the bar where there was also a long mirror edged with silver dollars.

'Here's your drink.'

I gave him five dollars. 'Darcy?'

He gave me two dollars change and served some-one else.

Ricky Gay finished singing 'Big Spender' and started to tell jokes. Another 10 per cent of the audience transferred their interest to companions and drinks. There was no music now but a few couples were dancing anyway. If the customer was always right the music would be starting up again pretty soon. I sipped the drink and considered my options: the barman I'd spoken to hadn't stopped working since. He hadn't winked or nodded at any-one to let them know about the snooper. He just wasn't interested. The other barmen and the wait-resses looked the same—too busy to care one way or the other. Somehow, I didn't think I'd get much co-operation from Ricky Gay.

A sign under a pair of buffalo horns over a door-way said 'Toilet'. I went through into a passageway that led to a door with a top-hatted silhouette on it at one end and to well-lit, imitation marble stairway at the other. I walked to the stairs; I still had the drink in my hand and when the man sitting at the top of the first flight stood up I raised my glass.

'Cheers,' I said.

He was a thickset character wearing a black T-shirt, jeans with a wide belt and basketball boots. He had a big bunch of keys swinging from the belt, too big to be anyone's actual set of keys.

'Other way, chum.' The voice was thick North Country British.

I leaned against the wall. 'What? What?'

'The pisser's at the other end of the passage. This's private up here.'

I swung around unsteadily, blinking. 'Doesn't say so.'

He came down the stairs confidently, unfastening the keys which were on a snap lock. The bunch was on several rings and looked as if it could be easily converted into a knuckle-duster or a mini-battleaxe. He was only about 30; too much fat bulged out above the belt, but he moved all right. He swung the keys lazily just below my nose. 'Piss off, chum.'

'Darcy here?' I spoke sharply and soberly and he was taken by surprise. He should have loaded his fist with the metal and punched but he went for another swing, intending to cut, and was too slow. I dropped the glass, whipped out the .38 and dug it into the midriff bulge. 'Drop the keys!' I dug hard as I spoke and he let the keys fall.

'A shooter. Come on . . .' He was going to get brave any minute. I brought my knee up hard and slammed it into his crotch. He groaned and sagged; I pushed with the gun and he sank down onto the stairs. He sat on broken glass and swore. He tried to move but I pinned him by putting the gun under his nose.

'Now look what you've done,' I said. 'You've cut yourself. You're going to have to be more careful. Darcy—where is he?'

His pudgy face was pale and it looked as if he'd bit his lip to add to his problems. He jerked his thumb over his shoulder. 'Up there.'

I gestured with the gun. 'Let's go.'

He eased himself up carefully, wincing and reaching behind him to pull the glass out. 'You're not a cop.'

'No. And you're not a nightwatchman. Take me up to Darcy.'

'He'll sort you.'

'We'll see. Your jeans are in a dreadful state.'

He went gingerly up the stairs; I followed two steps below and off to one side in case he had some idea of evening the score. He didn't. He went meek as a lamb along a carpeted corridor to the second of three doors, all of which had 'Private' written on them. He knocked.

'Who the hell is it?' The voice was rough, muffled and annoyed.

'Connelly.'

'Well?'

I showed Connelly my finger held to my lips. He opened his mouth and I dug him in the ribs with the gun.

'Connelly?' Less muffled now, closer to the door, but more annoyed. The door opened and the man in the photograph stood there; he'd put on weight and lost hair but he was unmistakably the same man. His white shirt was open to the waist showing a fleshy, hairy chest, tanned like his face and arms. I held the gun low and Darcy looked from Connelly to me, puzzled.

'Couldn't you handle it?'

'He's got a shooter,' Connelly said.

'And this.' I held up my licence. 'And this.' I put the licence away and pulled out the photographs. 'Tell Connelly here to go and find his keys and clean up the broken glass on the stairs. We have to talk.'

A woman appeared in the doorway behind Darcy. She was buttoning her blouse and straightening her tight skirt. Darcy saw my eyes flick to her but he could also see the gun now.

'Go on, Kenny; I'll deal with it.' Connelly turned and limped away; there was blood all over the seat of his trousers. Darcy looked amused.

'Sorry if I caught you at a bad time,' I said.

'Hardy, eh? I've heard of you.' He ran his hand over his thinning blonde hair, did up a button on his shirt and then patted his crotch. 'My fly's still done up, isn't it? Could've been worse. Come in, Hardy. Come in.'

9

I didn't exactly back Darcy into his own residence at the point of a gun, but I didn't treat him like my long lost brother either. What we were doing reminded me of an army training exercise—semi-serious. He retreated along the passage and I advanced. The woman circled around in the room we were headed for.

'The gun's a bit over the top,' Darcy said. 'You just had to ask.'

'I asked downstairs. Your staff's too busy serving watered drinks to be helpful.'

He smiled at that; he seemed to like smiling. 'What's this about?'

We were in a big living room now—white carpet, black leather armchairs and couch, glass and chrome bar and other fittings suggestive of the good, idle life. Outside the window the lights of Kings Cross became the lights of Elizabeth Bay and then became the lights of the yacht club and the marina and the boats at anchor. Darcy had done up a couple more buttons on his shirt, had pulled his stomach in and was over at the bar now making drinks. The woman stood beside him; she was tall and thin like a fashion model and with an appropriate lack of expression on her face. She'd got her blouse and skirt straight: she had short, bobbed blonde hair that hadn't become disturbed by whatever it was I'd interrupted. So she looked fine and that seemed to give her nothing else to do.

'Oh, Jackie,' Darcy said, 'this is Cliff Hardy. He's a private eye.'

She took her drink and didn't say anything. Darcy chuckled. 'You won't get much out of Jackie. I've never been able to decide whether it's because she hasn't got anything to say or because she thinks talking'll put lines on her face. Have a drink, full measure, and put that bloody gun away.'

I put the gun in my pocket and took out the photograph. I let Darcy put the drink on a table beside one of the armchairs. I hadn't had a full view of him while he made it and I've seen *The Maltese Falcon* three times. Ever since Gutman drugged Spade I've watched how the drinks are made. I put the photograph on the back of the couch beside a woman's silk-lined trench coat that was thrown across it. Half-covered by the coat was a leather shoulder bag with a nameplate reading 'Jackie George' on it. 'That's you in this picture, isn't it?' I said.

He had to take a few steps to look. He bent over, didn't touch it. 'Looks like it. So what?'

'Know the woman?'

He looked again and sipped his drink. 'Maybe.'

'Seen her lately?'

He shook his head. Just then, he wasn't smiling. His big, tanned face seemed to be deciding whether to set into an attitude of anger or amusement. In the end, it stayed neutral. He glanced across at Jackie who was sitting with her back straight, chin up, knees together, looking out the window expressionlessly. Her stillness and mine seemed to annoy Darcy; he swung around and raised his glass. 'To Jackie,' he said, 'the chatterbox.' He laughed. 'Come on, Hardy. What's this all about. Have a drink, man.'

I wanted a drink. I went over to the bar and poured some Scotch from the decanter into a glass. Darcy nodded approvingly as I squirted in some soda.

'That's the way. Now ...'

'I want information on the woman in that photograph.'

'Why?'

I drank some Scotch, considered telling him, but decided against it. It's all a horse-trade in this business, and he hadn't told me anything at all yet. 'Her name is Tania Bourke. Looks to me as if you two were on the way to something here.' I nodded at the photograph.

Jackie's eyes swung towards the couch. Just for a second and with no movement of the head. That was all, but I saw it. Darcy chuckled. 'I don't think so. Look, what is this? A few snaps of friends at lunch somewhere? I go to lunch every day. Sometimes I go twice a day, don't I Jackie?' He slapped his stomach as if to show the results. Jackie didn't respond except to finish her drink, stand up straight-legged and go over to the bar to make another. As she passed the couch she looked at the photograph.

'Maybe you know the man who took the picture?'

'Maybe. What is he? Some faggot in a pink shirt?'

'He's been described as ordinary. Wears a blue uniform.'

He spread his hands. 'I ask you. A cop, a parking attendant, petrol station guy? Hardy. I'm getting bored with this. I thought you'd be more interesting to meet.'

Something about his manner told me he was lying. He was alerted to danger. It was there in the body language—the way he raised his glass and pulled at the knee of his trousers. It was plain in the way he shot looks across at Jackie who'd resumed her statue impersonation. 'Maybe I can get something out of the Geordie,' I said. 'He probably scares the girls to death with those keys but ...'

'He's only been with me a year.' *Relief in the way he said it?* I thought.

'Yeah, this goes further back than that,' I said.

'Maybe two years, maybe three.' Jackie took a drink. I stood and collected the photograph. 'Well, I know you're lying but it'd be messy beating it out of you.' I put my glass back on the bar. 'Jackie'd get blood on her blouse and we'd have Connelly back here with his keys or worse. It doesn't seem worth it.'

'I think you made a mistake coming here, Hardy.'

'I don't think so. I enjoyed the show downstairs and the half Scotch. I enjoyed meeting Connelly. Hasn't been a total loss. Let me tell you, Darcy, you've got a lot of admirers.'

That *did* alarm him. 'What does that mean?'

'Goodnight, Jackie,' I said. I left them looking at each other as I crossed the room and opened the door. It wasn't much of an exit line but it would have to do. At least I'd discomfited Darcy and made Jackie move her eyes. And I'd had a drink. I felt like an under-achiever, but the coat and bag suggested to me that Jackie wasn't staying and therein lay possibilities.

No sign of Connelly in the hall or on the stairs. A few spots of blood though. The glass had been cleaned up. I went through the club, where the dancers and drinkers had taken control again, and up the stairs to the street. Exits and extrances are a little hard to find in that part of the city. Buildings can lead from one into another and you can come out half a block from where you went in. Not so with the Champagne Cabaret though. I prowled around the block, checking lights and doors, and couldn't see any cunning variations on in-at-the-front and out-through-the-back. I lurked in my car in the laneway behind the building and when Ricky Gay, wearing a leather jacket and jeans, was picked up by a fat man in a Mercedes sometime around 1 a.m., I was sure I was in the right place.

They came out about half an hour later—Jackie

and Connelly. She was wearing her trench coat and she trotted along as far away from Connelly as she could get. He looked around, stared at doorways or the steering wheels of cars. What he didn't know was that if you want to watch a place from a car and you don't want to be seen, you watch from the passenger seat or the back—where I was. They got into a white Volvo and headed east, Connelly driving.

He drove cars better than he intimidated and I had trouble keeping in touch in the back streets as he wove through the light traffic and caught the amber lights. I managed it though and was nicely positioned behind a couple of other cars as he turned off on the Darling Point side of Rushcutters Bay Park. It's top dollar country—big, well-maintained places crowding each other to compete for the fine view across the water to the city, and for the harbour breezes. And you could bet that any apartments would have security systems that'd hold up the SAS. More worrying were the cul-de-sacs which are common around there. Try following someone down a dead-end street and not look conspicuous and see how far you get. But the Volvo didn't get into the short streets with the blank endings; it turned into the heartland of the Point where the streets twist and turn but all go somewhere. It stopped in front of a big apartment block positioned between two mansions which were hidden behind palm trees and other luxuriant growth.

I drove past, made a tight turn and came back quickly along a high road that ran parallel to the other. From there I could see over the mansions to where the Volvo was parked, and the steep steps up to the apartment block. I stopped the car and focused my professional snooper's night glasses. Connelly escorted Jackie to the spotlit doorway of the apartments, where she used a key and went in without a nod or a thank you. There were eight storeys to the building, perhaps 30 apartments. A few lights were showing but it was clear where Jackie had come to rest—lights blazed in a couple of fourth-floor rooms suddenly and I thought I could see the movement of a curtain as she went out onto the balcony.

The Volvo moved off and I didn't try to keep it in sight. What I was looking for was a public telephone, hard to find in that high-rent, high-mortage district. When I did find one, at a crossroad that accommodated a tiny shopping centre, the compensation was that the directory, A to K was intact. I found George, J. listed with the right address and rang the number.

'Yes?'

'Jackie?'

'Yes. Who's this?' So she *could* talk, three words consecutively was definitely talking.

'This is Hardy. We met tonight.'

'Jesus.' Not anger in her voice—fear.

'Don't worry, I'm not watching you or anything. I followed you and Connelly to your place but now I'm miles away.'

'I . . . I can't talk to you.'

'But you want to, don't you?'

'I can't. What . . .?'

'What do I want? Information about Darcy. What's his full name?'

'Lionel. No . . . I can't . . .'

'Tell me about the woman in the photograph then.'

'I didn't know her.'

'Why did you react the way you did?'

'Jealousy. I'm going to hang up.'

'Wait, you were there that day but you didn't know what was going on. Is that what you're saying?'

'Between him and that bitch Bourke? Yes.'

'Who took the picture?'

'I don't know.'

'You do, Jackie. This is important. A couple of questions and I'll leave you alone. I won't involve you no matter what happens.' *Liar*, I thought. Bloody liar. This was one of the shitty moments.

'How many questions?'

My mind teemed with them. When had she last seen or heard of Tania Bourke? Where was the photograph taken? Who were the other people? Who was the photographer? 'Two,' I said.

'You promise?' she breathed, scarcely audibly.

'Yes.' *Shitty, very shitty.*

'All right.'

'Who was the photographer?'

'Joe Agnew took the picture. That's one.'

'A-g-n-e-w?' I spelled the name.

'Yes.'

'What's Darcy afraid of? Why the guy with the keys and the escort home for you and everything.'

'He's not afraid. You should be.'

'What did he say to you after I left?'

'That's three.' The phone clicked in my ear.

It was very late and I was tired. The car was reluctant to start, putting me in a bad temper which wasn't improved on New South Head Road by the early hours traffic—speeding Alfas and weaving Jags and not a cop in sight. I should have felt better about the night's work. Darcy was involved in something heavy and there was a connection through him to the Greenwich Apartments via Tania Bourke. Despite my promise, Jackie George could be a useful source of further information. And I had a name. All I had to do now was find what blue-shirted organisation Joe Agnew belonged to and I was on the trail. But the sluggish car and the tiredness and the fear in Jackie's voice made me sour. It made me think of how many different kinds of people wore blue shirts and how hard it might be to trace the photographer if he'd changed his name from something else, like Spiro did. And that was really depressing—the last I'd heard of Spiro Agnew was that he was rich and happy, like his former boss, advising, consulting and not admitting that he'd ever done anything wrong.

10

HOME around 3 a.m. The cat was sitting out in front of the house with an accusing look on its face. It stalked into the house ahead of me and went up the stairs. The house was quiet and the only light showing was in the kitchen; an anglepoise lamp burned on the bench and a letter from Helen sat in the circle of light:

Dear Cliff,

Woke up when you left and couldn't get back to sleep. Great movie—*Bermagui*, I mean. Gone for a drive and a think. I might drop in on Ruth at Balmoral and have an early breakfast with her at Mischa's. I will, in fact. At 7.30, say. Might see you? If not, later in the day.

love,
Helen

Ruth, a cousin of Helen's, had a flat overlooking Balmoral Beach. She was a clothes designer and the only woman I'd ever met who liked to drink white wine at breakfast. This was an old habit of mine which I gave up when I found that having a clear head until 6 p.m. wasn't the worst thing that could happen to you. Breakfast at Mischa's was one of the good Sydney things to do—I'd only tried it once but I could taste the scrambled eggs and the coffee that came from a bottomless pot. But my chances of making it were zero and I had the feeling that I
74

wasn't really welcome anyway. I followed the cat
upstairs and didn't even have the strength to kick it
off the bed.

I dreamed that Helen took flat one in the Greenwich Apartments. I was on stake-out, camped in a
tent in the courtyard around the clock, but couldn't
go inside. Very frustrating. Then she was living in
Ruth's flat at Balmoral. I had to climb hundreds of
steps up from the beach and the steps were made of
sand and kept crumbling under my feet. Also frustrating, and sweaty besides.

I woke up around eleven when the cat licked my
face. I rolled out, fed the cat, cleaned myself up and
looked at the morning paper while I drank coffee
very inferior to the stuff Helen would have had at
Mischa's. 'Talking up' seemed to be the key phrase;
everybody was talking up something—the economy,
Australian sport, the dollar. Trouble was, nobody
seemed to be doing anything, just talking.

The cat wanted to go out; it wouldn't come back
until it wanted more food and somewhere warm to
sleep. Great ecological niches, cats have carved out.
I got my notebook and looked through my information and expenses so far. That's one of the
rules that has to be observed from time to
time—check whether results and expenses are in
line. This time, it was hard to say. There were
threads hanging off the case. The usual procedure is
to pull the threads but this time I had a few too
many to pull and I didn't know which way they'd
run. Perhaps I'm getting conservative or maybe it's
just these clear-headed mornings—I decided to try
the institutions first.

The real estate agent had been alerted by Wise
that I would call, but he wouldn't say anything over
the phone. I drove to Newtown and virtually wasted
my time. He wouldn't say a lot over his desk either,
mainly because he didn't have much to say. Mr

Bushell was a bald man with glasses and a stammer. It was hard to imagine him high-pressuring anybody; maybe people bought houses from him because they felt sorry for him. He looked up from the thin file his secretary had brought in.

'Leased in 1981,' he said. 'Ran its course and then she rented month to month.'

'She?'

'Ms Tania Bourke,' he read.

'One name only? No mention of a tenant, no sub-let?'

He shook his head. 'We don't allow sub-letting. A boarder would be her business.'

'And the rent was paid how?'

'The way it is *still* being paid, directly from a bank. We're holding the receipts as we were instructed to do in ... ah ... 1982.'

'Must be quite a pile of 'em'.

He smiled and felt the skin on top of his head. 'Yes.'

'Does the money come from Ms Bourke's account?'

'I don't know. The draft we get just has an account number on it.'

'Which is?' I had the notebook out.

'S 4571.'

'And the bank?'

'Federation Bank.'

'Didn't you find this rather unusual, Mr Bushell? Two years and no contact between you and the tenant?'

He smiled again but this time he accompanied the smile with an adjustment of the glasses and left his skull alone. 'I'd call it ideal. No complaints, no requests for renovation, no late payment.'

'You're all heart.'

'It would have been awkward if Mr Wise had increased the rent, but he never did.'

I stood and put the notebook away. I was

76

suddenly glad I was a home owner, after a fashion, and not a renter. He went with me politely to the door. 'Mr Bushell,' I said, 'have you seen a woman named Helen Broadway in the last day or so? Looking for a flat or a small house?'

'No. To buy?'

'Could be.'

'I have a lovely place in Erskineville.'

I'd heard of lovely places in Erskineville—you have to walk along the railway tracks to reach them and use scuba gear to get into the kitchen. 'Thanks Mr Bushell. I'll let you know.'

Newtown still has a few pubs that remind me of the old days, when people weren't looking forward to the production of the cholesterol self-monitoring kit and checking the ph level before buying shampoo. As I walked along King Street, looking for one of these pubs, I remembered a Christmas lunch when an uncle of mine, the one who'd made all the money running the two-up at Tobruk, leant back in his chair and said to another uncle, the one who'd told me about getting orders to put Mills bombs in the pockets of German prisoners and refusing to do it: 'Great smoke, Neil, and a good beer.' They were both still alive, thanks to pacemakers and by-passes, while my teetotal father who'd worked in a munitions factory for most of the war, was long dead. 'Them's the skids', as the younger fry say.

I found the pub, ordered a light beer and a sand-wich and phoned the head office of the bank. Mr Carstairs would see me at 3 p.m. I ate and drank; I knew what Uncle Neil would think of the light beer—he'd cut railway sleepers for a living during the Depression and managed municipal swimming pools after the war. He probably wouldn't think much of Mr Carstairs either.

I put the Falcon in a car park in Kent Street and walked the couple of blocks to Martin Place. I had a newspaper clipping pinned up on a board at home that showed the route of the proposed monorail to run people between the Darling Harbour development and the city. I tried to imagine it, thin and noiseless on its slender pillars above Pitt Street, and I couldn't. I also couldn't decide whether I was for or against it. Not that it mattered; if the people who liked phrases such as 'high speed people mover' got their way we'd get the monorail and the citizens would just have to live with it. Like always.

I'd kept Leo Wise's cheque, drawn on the Federation Bank although not the head office, for just this purpose. Mr Carstairs of Customer Services looked at it and then at me with a fraction more interest. He was a thin, dark man who looked a lot like photographs of the young T. S. Eliot in a biography Helen was presently reading.

'Making inquiries for Mr Wise. Yes, I see.'

I read the number of the account from my notes and looked inquiringly at Mr Carstairs, who looked inquiringly back. 'I'm sorry,' he said. 'What exactly are you asking?'

'Whose account is this?'

'I'm sorry, I can't tell you that.' He took off his gold-rimmed spectacles and massaged the place on his nose where they sat. I wondered if T. S. Eliot did the same in between stanzas of *The Wasteland*.

'Why is that? We're talking about a few hundred dollars a month,' I said.

'Yes. Over several years, I understand. That is a considerable sum of money.'

Bankers are selective about what constitutes a considerable sum of money—they never use it when it's yours—say, when they make an accounting error. I held up Wise's cheque. 'It goes to Mr Wise eventually, surely as his agent . . .'

He shook his head. 'The bank cannot reveal such details.'

'What would it take to get them?'

'A Federal policeman might gain access with the right court order. Might.'

Suddenly, I got angry. Maybe it was the dreams, maybe the phony Swedish decor, maybe my dislike of T. S. Eliot. 'Look,' I said sharply. 'Did you know Mr Wise's daughter was gunned down in Kings Cross a couple of days ago?'

He looked shocked. 'No.'

'Yes. He'd be a big customer of yours, wouldn't he—Wise? I've seen his office. It's a bloody sight more impressive than this.'

'There's no need to be offensive.'

'Yes, there is. A twenty-year-old girl is dead and her father wants to know why. He's upset, understand? He wants to cut corners. He's not in a mood to be pissed around.'

Mr Carstairs arranged paper clips in front of him on his spotless white blotter. 'I see.'

'You're good at seeing. How are you at doing?' I read out the number again. 'Whose account is that?'

'I'd have to ask . . .'

'Don't ask anyone. Do something off your own bat for once.' I had him wavering and it was time to sweeten the pill. 'Look, Mr Carstairs, Leo Wise probably has lunch with some of your directors at City Tatts. If you help me I'll see that those directors learn from a satisfied customer that you're a man of judgement.'

His eyes slid sideways to his desk computer. 'What was that number again?'

I told him and he pressed keys. He watched the screen, rapt. I speculated on whether I should press my luck by coming around the desk to take a look. Decided against. 'Well?' I said.

'Joseph Agnew.'

I let out a long, slow breath. 'Ah hah.'

'Is that what you wanted to hear?'

'Maybe. Branch?'

He hit some keys. 'Newport Beach.'

I wrote it down so as to look keen. 'And do we have an address for Mr Agnew?'

He looked alarmed and took his hands away from the keyboard as if the fingers might go into business for themselves. 'I can't.'

'City Tatts,' I said. I mimed lifting a glass. 'Bright chap that Carstairs at Martin Place . . .'

Clickety, click. '2 Bougainville Street, Shetland Island.'

'Thank you, Mr Carstairs.'

11

I should have asked Carstairs whether Agnew's account was still active and several other things besides, but I thought I'd played the hand out. Movies were on my mind as I walked back to Kent Street. *Bermagui* and others: in *Desk Set* Tracy asks Hepburn what's the first thing she notices about a person and she answers 'Whether it's a man or a woman'. Obvious, but easily overlooked. I had that feeling about the case I was on now. That there was something entirely obvious about it that I hadn't seen. One of the troubles with this sort of feeling is that it leaves you uncomfortable but with no clues. I tried checking Angew, J., Shetland Island, in the telephone book, but there was no entry. One of the other troubles is that the feeling can be wrong—there may be nothing obvious and everything is just as confusing and complex as it appears.

Luckily, I don't have this feeling too often. For a private detective it amounts almost to incapacity. I phoned the house and told the recording machine that I'd be back later. I phoned Helen's cousin at Balmoral, got *her* recorded voice and told it nothing. This was done at a phone in the car park. I stood with the receiver in my hand wondering who I could try, to make it a recording machine hat-trick. I couldn't think of anyone and hung up. The abortive phoning had pushed my parking fee up into the next bracket. Poor Leo.

I nudged the expense sheet up further with a full

tank of petrol and set off for the peninsula. The trusty .38 was back in the kitchen drawer but I had the less trusty Colt .45 under the dashboard. I drove wondering why the thought of the gun had come to me. I don't believe in premonitions. Why couldn't I think of movies instead? *What did Woody Allen say was the only cultural advantage to be had in Los Angeles?* I was heading for the part of Sydney where the film people live—actors, writers, directors. They sit in the sun, sip wine, look out to sea and think of dark, threatening things to make movies about.

The Spit Bridge was up and I sat in a stream of waiting traffic, breathing the lead-laden air and considering my next moves. Agnew and his photographs were a key to something. For no good reason the thought came into my mind that there might be *two* dead women in the case. Maybe Agnew had killed Tania Bourke. Why? And why leave a flat paid for and vacant for years? Maybe Tania Bourke had killed Agnew. Maybe Lionel Darcy had killed them both, *and* Carmel Wise. I decided this was mental babble. I found Bougainville Street in the Gregory's and worked out that the best way to get to Shetland Island was to hire an outboard in Bayview. Practical steps, no theory. The bridge opened and I concentrated on my driving.

I hadn't been to the Bayview marina for a few years. They'd had a fire since then and things had changed a little; there was new timber and fresh paint around; aluminium had replaced some of the rusted iron railings. The place had moved with the times: the shop was new and the emphasis on windsurfing equipment was very new. At the office my Bankcard and driver's licence got me a runabout with a big Johnson outboard. A young, sleek woman handled the boat hire and turned me over to a heavily built, middle-aged man who looked as if he belonged to the previous, less smart days at the marina.

'Going over to Shetland?' he said as he helped me with the boat.

'Right.'

'Know people over there?'

We had the boat at the bottom of a short ladder and I dropped into it, feeling it rock, and adjusting. 'Fellow named Agnew,' I said. 'Joe Agnew. Know him?'

He shook his head and unlooped the rope. 'Nope. Have a good trip.'

'Hold on. Look, this is just on spec. I don't really know this bloke but I want to have a word with him. He's a bit younger than me, smaller. Dark, I think. I'm told he wears a blue uniform sometimes.'

He scratched his stubbled chin. 'Well, you know, I've been here for donkey's years. They come and go. Lot go by ferry. I don't think I know anyone like that.'

'He's a photographer. Probably carries a camera, maybe a couple of cameras, lenses and that.'

More chin scratching and then he gave a tug on the rope that almost upset me. 'Yes, sure. Now you mention it. There was a feller like that. Took photographs. He worked for the Customs someone told me.'

'Customs! Yeah, that fits. Have you ever talked to him?'

'Me? Nah, just seen him around, you know. But not lately. Not for a few years at least. I don't think you'll find him there now, mate.'

'Never mind,' I said. 'I'll have a look anyway.' He threw me the rope. 'Thanks for the help.' He nodded—he thought I meant help with the boat. I started the motor and took the boat out into the channel. Shetland Island is about two miles from Bayview. The island is roughly circular, very roughly, and about a mile across. I'd only been there once and that was for a picnic as a kid, about 30 years back. I remembered a park in the middle of the island, a lot of bush and nothing much more.

It was late in the afternoon and cool on the water. I'd put on a zipped jacket to give me a deep enough pocket to put the Colt in, but I was glad of it now for the warmth. Navigation was simple: the island was there, dead ahead over the slightly choppy water. All I had to do was head for it. Landing might be a bit tricky: were there beaches, a public wharf, private jetties? I didn't know.

In other circumstances it would have been a pleasant run. Some yachts looked graceful off to the east and I was passed by a cabin cruiser also heading for Shetland Island. The helmsman gave me a wave which I returned as I bounced across his wake. The breeze whipped at my hair and the spray stung my eyes but I wasn't in the mood for the beauties of aquatic nature. If Agnew was a Customs officer that made sense of the entries in the notebook. K was KLM, Q was Qantas, P was Pan American and so on. The numbers referred to flights and the other letters to pieces of luggage. I didn't think that Joseph Agnew was on the lookout for native birds or Aboriginal artefacts.

The island, green in the distance, was multi-coloured closer up. I could see houses on the hills, roads paved and unpaved and different kinds of foliage. The side I approached first was rocky with a light surf beating against the cliffs. I kept well back and circled to the east. There was an indentation in the coast which offered some protection which jetty builders had taken advantage of. Several wooden structures edged out from the beach; there were some boats at anchor between them and others tied up to the piles. Gulls circled overhead and swooped down to duck their beaks under the deep green water. More natural beauty I had no use for. I turned the boat towards the largest of the jetties, cut the motor too far out and had to drift in with oar at the ready to prevent bumping. Off to the right, a couple of houses occupied a short promontory; they were half-surrounded by water and I could see rough timber walls and low, long verandahs. Great spot to get away from it all, if you had a hundred thousand bucks not working.

No-one challenged my right to tie up at the jetty. A couple of people were working on their boats, a few were lounging on theirs, and I wasn't worth their attention. That suited me fine. I had the simple map of the island in my head: outer ring road; inner ring road with several streets radiating off it towards the park in the centre; and one road bisecting the island. Bougainville Street was one of the radials. I reached the outer road by stepping off the end of the jetty right onto it. It was a wide, well-made road with a narrow gravel strip on either side. Things had changed on the island since little Cliff's visit in the faraway fifties. It was the smells that brought the memories back—gum trees, perhaps a peculiar combination of them, intermingled with the smell of cut fennel where someone had been mowing an unruly lawn. There were many more houses now and more big ones. The outer road had been a rutted dirt track back then and it seemed that we hiked for hours to get to the park. Not so now; the road had been graded and followed the contours of the land easily; it was uphill to the bisecting road, but gently. As I walked I got glimpses of the water through the trees and eventually over the tops of them. It was going to be a soft, mild night with a breeze. The treetops waved and the water turned darker. *Christ*, I thought, you'll be admiring the sunset next. You're here to work!

From the road I could see an untidier part of the

island, down near the water's edge where small, old houses clustered together like bits of driftwood. Up here it was all solid constructions and cement driveways. A football came sailing towards me as I walked past one of the houses. I caught it awkwardly, surprised at its shape. It was an American football, smaller than the ones I was used to, and pointed.

'Throw it!' The order came from a kid standing twenty feet away. I could see him through the sticks of a high tea-tree fence. It's an old habit—when told, asked or challenged to throw or jump something, the odds are I'll do it. I'd seen the quarterbacks on TV; the way they gripped the ball, shuffled and threw. I tried it: the ball sailed in a perfect, looping spiral into the kid's hands.

'Hey,' he cried. 'You're good!'

He threw it back in the same way and I caught it again.

'Just luck,' I said. We both approached the fence. 'You don't sound like an American,' I said.

'My Dad is.'

'I see. D'you play baseball too?'

'Naw. Prefer cricket.'

An all-round kid. 'Am I heading the right way for Bougainville Street?'

'Yeah. It's up there.' He pointed.

'Know a man named Agnew who lives in that street?'

'Naw. It's a crummy street. You wanna have another throw?'

'One more.'

He tossed the ball over and turned his back to the fence. He was a stocky kid wearing jeans and a Dallas Cowboys T-shirt. He was strong-looking, with an air of concentrating on the job at hand. 'You yell "hike",' he said. 'I run back. You count three and then throw. Try to throw straight and keep it away from that fuckin' bush over there. Okay?'

86

'Okay.' I felt silly. 'Hike!' I said.

The kid ran; I counted and threw. The ball wobbled and looked like falling short. The kid spun around, dived and caught it inches above the grass. I raised both hands in the American athletes' salute, felt the gun bump against my ribs, and walked on.

Bougainville Street let the rest of the area down badly. For one thing it straggled and dog-legged where the other streets were straight. For another, the houses had more fibro cement in them and less timber and brick than was the rule. Number 2 was at the bottom of the range—a wide bungalow set back in an over-grown garden. The fence in front was a ruin and the grass had become tangled and matted at about knee height. The gate hung at a crazy angle and I stepped around it and went up the path, scarcely discernible in the grass, to the front door. No deep, shady verandahs here; just a mean little structure of rotting timber and rusty iron, over-hanging the front door.

The houses on either side were better tended but had the look of weekenders, infrequently visited. This was Friday; maybe there'd be neighbours in residence tonight, maybe not. Across the street from this house and the few on either side of it, the land fell away too sharply to allow building. It was the perfect setting for a house to be left empty, neglected and ignored. I wouldn't say I was disappointed; I hadn't expected Agnew to be out there mowing the lawn, but the neglect looked discouragingly old. Still, you never can tell. A man on the bottle lets things slip; the desertion could be contrived rather than real; or things might look different around the back.

I pushed the gate further open and walked to the front door. There were two wooden steps in front of it, one of which disintegrated when I stepped on it. A heavy knock brought no response other than to cause more paint to flake off the door. The glass in

87

the transom was cracked and mended with insulating tape. Blinds were drawn down over the two front windows. I walked down the side of the house pushing aside stalks of woody weeds that jutted up from the fence and from the foundations of the house itself. One consolation, I told myself—no dog.

Behind the house the neglect intensified. The outhouse toilet was a ruin; some of its boards had collapsed, letting in the weather and the weeds. A rusted bicycle with cobwebs growing all over the frame and between the spokes was propped up against the back of the house. The three or four wooden steps up to the door were rickety; the second one almost broke when I put an experimental foot on it. The door was even more decayed than the one in the front. The windows were yellow with dust and fly specks and the frames were dry and splintered like old paling fences. The grass was waist-high and big oleander and privet bushes grew, higher than the fences, along both sides of the backyard. The only thing that had stopped growing was the decrepit Hills hoist.

The door was locked. A little effort with the fingertips pulled the window catch away from the wood. I slid the lower section up an inch and felt the absence of a sash. I let it down, fossicked for a piece of wood in the yard and found one the right length. I propped the window open, moved the bike across, stood on the crossbar and climbed through.

12

IT had been a long time since any fun had been had in that house, if you don't count cockroaches. There was a thick film of dust over everything—furniture, books, crockery, glassware. The place looked as if it had been left suddenly, one busy morning maybe, and had never been returned to. The covers on the double bed in the larger of the two bedrooms had been quickly pulled up. A single bed in the other room had been used as a linen store—sheets and clothes, roughly folded, were stacked on it. A man's clothes and a woman's, like those in the drawers and wardrobe of the other bedroom.

Dishes had been washed at the sink and left to drain. Dust settling on them when wet had formed a sludge that was now a thin layer of dried mud. It was an uncanny and uncomfortable feeling to go through the drawers and cupboards collecting papers and other scraps of the lives that had been lived here. The clothes were the firmest evidence: blue shirts, dark trousers, plain shoes. There were holes where a badge had been pinned. Among the man's clothes there was also some beach gear and summer wear. I found a camera and light meter but no photographs. The woman's clothes were the kind Tania Bourke would have worn when she wasn't strutting her stuff in the city—still well-made, still man-attracting, but with some concessions to a relaxed life in the lower heels and more casual styles.

As the flat in the Greenwich Apartments had contained more of the woman's things, this held more of the man's. The paperbacks tended to be of the hairy-chested variety, Robert Ruark and co. There was a small collection of the sort of thing that had been contraband in Australia until the Whitlam enlightenment—*Lady Chatterley, Portnoy*, Henry Miller etc. Joe Agnew must have been assiduous in his duties, or perhaps the boys divided the confiscated hot stuff at the pub after work.

I worked through the house thoroughly as the light dimmed outside. The electricity and gas were connected. The water ran rusty, the colour of weak tea. In the end I could probably have filled another garbage bag with Agnew's and Bourke's significant effects. I could certainly have proved that the same two people had occupied this house and flat one at the Greenwich Apartments. Some newspapers and magazines indicated activity later than in the other place, up to about a year ago. Unusually for that sort of house, the front door had a letter slot. Mail had built up inside the door like an Aboriginal midden. Most of it was unsolicited junk, none of it was revealing, personal, or intimate, but receipted power bills indicated that someone was paying the way in a place where no-one lived. Again.

'Where have you gone?' I said to myself aloud. The sound of my own voice startled me. I was in the living room which was almost dark. I switched on the light and heard a scurrying behind the couch against the wall. *A fully paid up house for mice*, I thought. Wait till the news gets around. I turned on the three-in-one sound system and hit the AM button. After a few bars of music I got the seven o'clock news. They were shooting white people in the Lebanon, brown people in the Philippines and black people in South Africa. Petrol and unemployment were up, farm incomes and the dollar were

90

down. Two Balmain players were suspended for head-high tackling and tomorrow was going to be wet. No comfort anywhere.

I left the radio on and wandered through the house wondering if I should make an attack on the floorboards. In the front bedroom the blind was torn at the side and I glanced through the gap.

A man was standing in front of the house; he was slightly bent to get some cover from a shrub and the way his right hand was positioned suggested to me that he was holding a gun. He squinted at the house and then turned and made a beckoning gesture with his left. I raced through the house to the back, turned the key and pulled the door open. I was reaching for my gun when a man who already had one out and at the ready stepped into view. He lifted the gun.

'Stand right there.'

I froze; he moved forward and gestured for me to back away. I stood my ground; he was going to come up the steps and that was fine with me. When the second step took his weight it crumbled; he lurched sideways and I bulled forward straight into him. He lost balance and footing; his gun slammed into the side of the house and I was past him and running through the thick grass to the back fence. I think I would have tried to jump it if I'd had to, but a ten-foot section of it had fallen flat. I hurdled the remains and ran on.

The light was fading fast now and the going was difficult. I was in light scrub and heading upwards. A rabbit track zigzagged up the hill and I followed it as best I could. Zigzagging was fine if there was going to be any shooting from behind. I gasped and wheezed, grabbed at saplings to keep moving up in the rockiest and roughest bits, and I didn't look back. You can tell when you're being pursued; you feel it on the back of your neck like a cold breeze and

I was feeling it now. Still no shooting though.

I realised that I was heading towards the park in the middle of the island and I tried to remember its layout. Too long ago, and they'd probably filled in the water holes and installed adventure playgrounds. It wasn't the brightest prospect—in the gathering gloom with at least three men and two guns after me, I should have been looking for human support rather than a tree patch with possums.

I blundered on, tripping on tree roots and feeling branches cut my face. I tasted blood and almost fell when a branch hit my right eye solidly and squarely. Suddenly, I was half-blind. Everything to the right of centre was a blank. I felt a rush of fear and blinked frantically but the vision wouldn't clear. I swung my head to increase the field of sight and almost fell. I felt useless all down the right side. I was barely moving when I finished the climb and reached a level, grassy stretch. I stood for a minute with heaving chest, blind eye and raw throat, trying to decide what to do next. I could see the lights of the houses below me and hear noises: with diminished vision, the noises were incredibly clear—birds, rustling animals, stealthy feet. I jogged across the clearing towards a stand of trees. The eye throbbed; I put my hand up to it and felt a blow on the back of my neck. I sagged, dug in my pocket for the gun and felt it again in the same spot but harder. I closed the other eye. I didn't want to but I couldn't help it. I fell forward, slamming my shoulder into the hard earth.

I didn't pass out but I might just as well have. I had trouble getting the good eye open; my shoulder hurt and I had practically no breath in my lungs so I lay as if I was paralysed. Three men stood over me—the two I'd seen back at the house and one other. The two I'd seen before were breathing hard, the other

wasn't, but all six of their eyes were open and none seemed to have a mouthful of blood like me. I managed to turn my head sideways and spit out some of the blood.

'Christ,' the one I'd seen at the front of the house said.

'He's all right.' This was from the third man who wasn't out of breath, wore a smart, full-length coat in contrast to the casual clothes of the others, and seemed to be the one in charge.

The man I'd pushed past on the back steps rubbed his shoulder. One small score to Hardy. 'Do we do it?' he said.

The boss bent down and took my gun from the jacket pocket. He put it away in his coat. 'That's what they tell us.'

'Do what?' I mumbled. 'Who are you?'

'Shut up!' The boss snapped. 'Think you can walk?'

'How far?' I said.

'Not far.' He turned on his heel. 'If he can't walk, don't try to carry him. Drag him!'

They pulled me up; everything spun and then settled down into a swirling mist. Maybe I walked, maybe they dragged me. I felt as if I was swimming while standing upright. I don't know how far it was to the car, probably not far, but it felt like five miles. I knew it couldn't be because the island was only one mile across. I didn't care, it still felt like five. Sitting in the car felt good. I was in the back with my two friends beside me—soft seat, back rest; when the car got going I buckled in the middle and vomited on the floor between my legs.

The one on my right said, 'You animal!' and belted me across the face. The damaged eye took some of the force of the blow and I yelled with the pain.

'Next time swallow it,' he said.

'I'll make you eat it if I get the chance,' I said.

'You won't, Hardy.'

That gave me two things to ponder—they knew my name and they were going to 'do' something with me. I concentrated on getting my breath back and my right eye open on the short drive. I succeeded with the first but not with the second. The flesh around the eye was puffy and swollen and I felt as if I'd lost muscle control in that part of my face. The shoulder hurt too; it was dislocated or nearly so. I was in poor shape for running away or fighting or doing anything but talking. I was so worried about the eye that I couldn't think of anything to say. Then I stopped worrying about the eye; dead is dead, one eye or two. I *had* to talk.

The car stopped at the jetty. We sat awhile for my companions to make sure the coast was clear. Then the boss snapped his fingers. 'Harry,' he said. 'Take his boat.'

'I'll lose my deposit.'

'Shut up!'

Harry, who hadn't spoken yet, said 'Right.' He got out of the car and vanished. The boss and the other man manhandled me along the jetty and down a set of steps into a boat—a speedboat with sleek lines and an enclosed cabin in front. They switched on lights, started the engines and took her expertly out into the channel. I heard a Johnson engine kick a couple of times before it started. My boat. There was no-one around to yell to. I couldn't have made it over the side and I doubted I could swim with the damaged shoulder anyway. *Talk, Hardy*, I thought. Talk!

'Tell me what's going on,' I said.

No reply.

Were they going to drop me in the water? I felt the fear stir inside me and looked around for the right stuff—wire, cement blocks, bed frames, but there was nothing like that.

My voice sounded as if it was coming from underwater already. 'Who's behind this?' I said. 'Darcy?'

The boss was sitting opposite me with his coat hitched up over his knees. He was a tall, thin character with a grooved, sharp-boned face. The grooves looked as if they were cutting their way through to the bones.

'In a way,' he said. 'Any problems. Rolf?'

The man at the wheel lit a cigarette. 'No,' he said. Not a gabby pair.

'D'you want a cigarette, Hardy?' the boss said.

I shook my head which hurt. 'Bad for the health,' I said, 'but probably not as bad as meeting up with you guys.'

'That's right,' he said. 'You're in a bad way. Eye looks terrible.'

Then he shut up and looked out across the water. I was puzzled by them; they didn't act like hoods but then, hoods aren't always acting like hoods these days. The boss had a kind of hard-bitten dignity and Rolf was cool and relaxed at the wheel as if what he was doing was perfectly legitimate. *Cops?* I wondered and the thought gave me no comfort.

'Where're we going?' I said.

'You're Sydney born and bred, aren't you, Hardy? You should know. Have a look.'

I swivelled around on the hard seat painfully and tried to get my bearings. The sky was dark now, but the moon was up and there were lights dotted here and there all around. Shetland Island lay to the east and we were heading towards a dark coastline.

'National Park,' I said.

'You sound relieved.'

'I thought this might be a burial at sea without the flag and the gun salute.'

He gave a short, barking laugh. 'You're a romantic, Hardy. Forget about Davey Jones' locker. Haven't you heard of the shallow grave in Kuringai Chase?'

'Yeah, I've heard of it. I wouldn't call that method reliable.'

'No? That's interesting.'

'Getting close,' Rolf said.

We entered a bay that seemed to taper in to a stream that disappeared into darkness. Before we reached the mouth of the stream Rolf cut the motor and the boat drifted in the current.

'Dinghy, Hardy,' the boss said.

'Jesus. Why don't you just shoot me now and drop me over?'

'Too easy. Come on.'

We stood at the stern and watched a rowboat approach us.

'Williamson?' The whisper came from the boat, only just audible over the plopping oars.

'Yes. You're taking two. Okay?'

' 'kay. Here we are. Steady . . .'

Williamson swung his long legs over the side and lowered himself into the boat. I moved awkwardly and Rolf helped me roughly to do the same. I squatted in the boat; my shoulder was on fire and my eye throbbed and gave me stabs of pain at the smallest movement. It was hard to hold my head steady in the moving boat and I eventually used both hands to help me do it.

The boatman pulled hard against the last of a running tide and we moved steadily up the stream. It was wider in some spots than others; branches from the trees hung over the water and a couple of times Williamson told me to duck. I did so and groaned at the pain. After about ten minutes of rowing we ran ashore on a narrow, sandy beach. The boatman heaved the vessel far enough up to allow himself and Williamson to jump onto dry sand. I couldn't jump.

'Get your feet wet, Hardy,' Williamson said. 'It's part of the treatment.'

I didn't know what to make of that but I eased

gingerly over the side and waded to land through a few inches of water.

'What now?' I said.

'Short walk. You can wait here,' he said to the boatman. 'I can handle this.' He produced a torch from his coat pocket and took out his gun almost as an afterthought. He was cool and confident which made everything feel very much worse. He pushed my damaged shoulder and I yelled.

'Sorry. That way.' He flashed the torch beam at the scrub. I could just see a break in it. My vision was good in the open eye but it's hard to gauge distance and levels with only one eye. I stumbled a lot as I walked which hurt the eye and shoulder. My feet, sloshing about in wet shoes and socks, were cold. Once or twice Williamson jabbed me with his gun but he was a pro. He moved around from side to side and dropped back sometimes so that I never really knew where he was—not that I could have done anything about it anyway.

We came out of the scrub into a sandy hollow, like the space between two big sand dunes. The grass was thick over the area. Two men stood to one side, just out of the scrub. One held a hurricane lantern and I could see a rake and a broom on the ground beside him. I shivered and stopped. Williamson moved around and stood beside me. He extended the hand that held the torch. 'I want you to look very carefully to where this is shining, Hardy. What do you see?'

I stared through the darkness trying to keep my restricted vision inside the area lit by the torch. The eye watered and I rubbed it. 'Nothing,' I said.

He moved the torch. 'There. Can't you see anything?'

I could. Just discernible were two long, narrow disturbances of the earth. The grass had partially grown over them but you could see the slight rise of

97

the ground, like long lumps, the slight shadow.

'What is it?' I said.

I felt Williamson's gun muzzle touch the back of my neck. It rested there lightly. It was cold and I could smell the faint tang of gun oil.

'There lie Joe Agnew and Tania Bourke,' Williamson said.

13

A rake, I thought. What good is a rake. Where's the shovel?

Williamson took the gun away and turned me around back towards the track. He used the gun to steer me but he prodded the undamaged side. 'Little charade, Hardy. I'm a Federal policeman. Narcotics. Teach you to mind your own fucking business.'

I felt some warmth creep back into my cold, stiff, tingling body.

'God,' I said. 'I thought . . .'

'Yeah. You held up pretty well.' He swung the torch beam over footprints and other marks in the sandy soil. 'Clean her up, boys. Just like she was.'

I stumbled back to the beach and got my feet wet again getting in the boat. Williamson gave me some of the details as we made the trip back to the speed-boat and some more on the run to Bayview.

'Agnew and Bourke were part of a big drugs operation,' he said. 'Bourke was a courier. Have you worked out what Agnew's part was?'

'Yes,' I said. My eye was hurting like hell and it was all a charade. Still, I had to play along. I didn't know what Williamson's complete plan was; there was still time and opportunity for him to erase me. 'He was in at the Customs end. He watched for cetain flights and bits of luggage. I don't know how they'd have worked it. All that stuff looks pretty random to me when I've travelled.'

'It is, or it can be. If you've got the luggage handlers and some of the Customs men fixed it's less random. It was complicated but it works. Worked.'

'What happened?' We were back in the speedboat now, a smoother ride than the dinghy but not smooth enough for me. 'Haven't got anything to drink on you, by any chance?'

'No. The usual thing happened. People got greedy, started to cheat. We got someone inside and looked like cracking it.'

'Where does Darcy fit in?'

'He's an informer . . .'

'Which means he's a dealer as well.'

'Set a thief. He knew Bourke and Agnew. Knew Bourke pretty well, in fact.'

'Yeah, his girlfriend's not too happy about that.'

He shrugged his well-tailored shoulders. 'He knows it. His problem.'

Rolf handled the wheel like an artist. The shore lights were coming up fast—the trip back always seems shorter than the one out. Soon there'd be people around instead of dark stretches of water, telephones not trees. I would have felt better if I'd been able to see properly. As it was, the blanked-out eye felt like a hot coal in my head, but there were still things I needed to know.

'Who killed them?' I said.

'The man who was trying to take over from the big man.'

'When?'

The boat bumped the piles; Rolf tossed the ropes, jumped to the jetty and tied us up. He stood and lit a cigarette. He was a bit of a specialist, Rolf. 'This all happened a while back,' Williamson said. 'Don't trouble yourself. Look, can you get up here? Ladder's awkward.'

'I can do it.' I climbed onto the marina walkway. My boat was tied up where they'd be able to see it from the office in the morning. I was dizzy and the shoulder and eye injuries made me feel as if I'd taken a hard left-right combination. I hung on to the handrail all the way back to dry land.

'The thing is this,' Williamson said. 'Oh, I've got someone to drive you home. Don't worry about it.'

'I won't lick your boots either.'

He ignored that, intent on his story. 'Bourke had got hold of a big shipment. She diverted it. Agnew helped. They got killed. The big man's still looking for them and the stuff.'

'Who is he?'

He shook his head. 'Can't tell you. But you know him. Everyone knows him. He's getting close. When he moves to get the stuff we'll get him. That's all you need to know.'

'Like hell, it is! Jesus.'

'Sit down in the car. Come on.' He led me to the Falcon and helped me in. Then he put my Colt in the glove box. Rolf was hanging around and Williamson turned to him. 'Got anything to drink? Brandy or something?'

Rolf shook his head. 'Got a joint.'

'That'd be right,' Williamson said. 'Hardy, any use to you?'

'No. What about the flat in the Cross and the house over there?'

'Part of the set-up. We've left them as they were. Keep an eye on them.'

'You know how I got into this?'

'Yeah, the girl who got killed outside the Greenwich place.'

'Well?'

'We had nothing to do with it.'

'Nothing?'

'Well, only after the fact. We passed the word to the police not to ... disturb things. You have my word, Hardy.'

I snorted. 'Shit, what's that worth?'

'Suit yourself. All I'm saying is that we had nothing to do with the girl's death and it was completely unconnected with our operation. Completely.'

'Why the hell couldn't you have just told me this?'

'Darcy told us how you acted when you broke in on him. The girlfriend told us about the phone call. You were getting warm, right?'

'I suppose so.'

'We knew you'd get somewhere at the bank, one way or another. Or somewhere along the line. If you'd looked into the leasing of the house on the island you'd have been led somewhere else. Another house. It's the way they lived. The trail's there to be followed. I mean that's *why* it's there. And we didn't need you tramping around on it.'

'Still . . .'

'Still nothing. You've got a reputation, Hardy. You know what for?'

'Sustaining physical damage?'

'Stubbornness. I was told I'd have to convince you. You looked pretty convinced back there in the park. Are you convinced, Hardy?'

'I'm convinced,' I said.

'Rolf'll drive you home. You'll have to get that eye seen to. It looks pretty bad.'

Book Two

14

I don't know what time it was when I got home. I was barely conscious. Rolf got me into the house and Helen set to work with hot water and cotton-wool. She phoned Ian Sangster who left his Friday night bridge game to come.

'Christ,' he said. 'You look like you've gone a few rounds with Fenech.'

'Try a tree,' I said. 'Or more precisely, a branch. How bad is it, Ian?'

He put his bag of tricks down, took out one of the medieval instruments they use, and examined the eye closely. 'It looks bad, Cliff. You need a surgeon. I'll get you into hospital tonight and with luck I can get one of the best men in Sydney on it tomorrow.'

'*One* of the best?' Helen said.

'It's a competitive field. They argue about it. Why's he sitting all hunched like that?'

I was on the couch in the front room still wearing my jacket because I couldn't move the arm enough to slip it off. Helen's attempt to do so had called forth an unmanly scream. I'd taken off the wet footwear though. 'Shoulder,' I said.

'Jesus, Cliff, you're . . .'

'I know. Too old. I'm too old, Helen.'

'You're babbling. He wants whisky, Ian. What d'you reckon?'

'Why not? It has important medicinal qualities. I'll take some of the same medicine. Let's have a look at the shoulder.'

'After the Scotch,' I said. I had a stiff one and heard about the hand Ian had been holding when Helen called. I had another and hardly screamed at all as he eased the jacket off.

'You could almost do the Elephant Man,' Ian said. 'With the eye like that and the back all swollen.'

'Thanks,' I said. 'Quasimodo'd be more like it. It feels like a hump.'

'Richard III, then,' Ian said. 'Don't go down-market.'

'You're both crazy,' Helen said. 'It's bloody blue!'

'Bruised.' Ian finished his whisky and tapped the glass. 'More, if you please. This the first time you've seen him like this, Helen?'

'Yes.'

'You're lucky. Cyn ...'

'Ian!' Pain shot through me as I spoke. 'Drop it, Ian.'

'No. Tell me.' Helen poured more whisky for Ian and one for herself. I nodded and she added a few drops to my glass. Ian was probing at the shoulder; his hands were cool and firm. It almost felt better under them.

'This is dislocated and strained. Nothing broken, I think. He was a wild boy in those days, I can tell you. Liked to mix it, would you believe? I stitched him and set him in plaster. Quite often.'

'No good for the sex life,' Helen said.

'Funny, that's what Cyn used to say.'

'D'you mind?' I said. I felt myself slowing down and drifting, stress and Scotch will do that to you. 'Shouldn't you ring this fuckin' wizard of micro-surgery ... whatever?'

Ian was fiddling with a syringe and a bottle with a rubber membrane on the top. 'Blah, blah mls of scotch whisky, blah, blah mls of this,' he mused. He gripped and pressed until a vein stood up in my arm. He slid the needle in. 'Goodnight, Cliff. I promise to respect your woman.'

106

I woke up in a private hospital in Hunter's Hill. I didn't know then that it was Hunter's Hill, but the water and trees and gracious rooftops I saw from the window told me that it sure as hell wasn't Glebe. I was wearing a nightshirt—something that had lain in a drawer since the last time I was in hospital, about eight or nine years back—long stubble and a plastic bangle around my wrist with my name on it and some coded things I couldn't understand. My watch was on the bedside table. It was 7 a.m. on Saturday: time to lie in bed with Helen and read the papers, check the quotes of the week and if there was a movie on we wanted to see. No Helen.

A nurse came around at 7.30 and took my pulse and temperature.

'When's breakfast?' I said.

'Tomorrow for you.'

'Eh? What is this, the Gulag?'

'You're fasting, Mr Hardy. You're being operated on at ten o'clock.'

I realised for the first time that I was only looking through one eye. The other was closed, covered with a pad and throbbing. Through one eye, the nurse looked fresh, clean-scrubbed and young. *Invisible Man* jokes, *Prisoner in the Iron Mask* jokes, wouldn't mean a thing to her. My shoulder was stiff but not as sore as it had been. I wriggled up in the bed. 'What am I being operated on for, nurse?'

'Torn cornea.'

'It sounds like a rock group,' I said. A soft, warm wave called sleep hit me in the face and I slid down the bed and off it onto a soft, warm cloud.

The next time I awoke, two men in white gowns were bending over me. One was looking at my eye, the other was asking me my name.

'Cliff Hardy,' I said.

'How did you sustain this injury?'

'I ran into a tree branch.'

'My name is Stivens, Mr Hardy. I'm a surgeon.

The sight of your right eye is endangered but the operation I am going to perform has a 90 per cent success rate. Do you understand?'

'What d'you like at Randwick in the fifth?'

'I beg your pardon.'

'It sounded like you were quoting odds.'

'Yes, Ian Sangster told me you have a sense of humour. I have not. This is Dr McGregor, he is an anaesthetist. I believe he has a sense of humour too.'

The other white-gowned figure nodded and grinned. 'Dr Stivens,' I said.

'Mister.'

'Mister Stivens. Could you just hold out your hands for a second. Like this?'

'I told you I have no sense of humour.'

'Please.'

He held out both hands; dark hairs sprouted around his wrists. I let myself go back and relax. 'I'm sorry about the sense of humour,' I said, 'but in your case I'll settle for the steady hands.'

'Dr McGregor?' Stivens said.

'You'll feel a prick, Mr Hardy. Then I'll count backwards from ten and at five I'll tell you a joke. Ten, nine, eight . . .'

I didn't hear the joke.

It was a private room. I'd never had a private room in a hospital before. I couldn't have afforded it. I couldn't afford it now. Helen and Sangster were there. *Where's the cat?* I thought. But you know cats, they're never around when you need them.

'How does it look?' I said. 'Get it? Eye operation? Look?'

'Jesus,' Helen said.

'You must never touch narcotics, Cliff,' Sangster said. 'They'd be too nice for you.'

'Okay,' I pulled my right hand out from under the bedclothes and put it up to my eye. Big patch, very tender. Helen gently took my hand away and held it. Her fingers were cool and smooth. I played with them. Sangster cleared his throat and stood.

'Vance Stivens'll be back tonight,' he said.

'Vance?'

'That's right. He told me to tell you he'll adjust the sutures under local anaesthetic tonight.'

'Terrific,' I said. 'I hope he's had a nice day.'

'We played golf this morning after he'd worked on you.'

'Good. What did he shoot?'

'Eighty-one. He'll be happy with that.'

'I'm glad.' I gripped Helen's hand and felt a strong sexual urge. Sangster moved away from the bed.

'He also said to tell you that when he's finished it'll feel like there's a house brick under your eyelid. That'll last for a couple of weeks. You're not to worry.'

'I won't. Thanks, Ian.'

'Ciao.'

Helen was wearing a silk dress I liked and she smelled wonderful. Our hands were gripped together.

'Not much we can do about it here. When do I get out?'

'Tomorrow. But you could be on hand jobs only, for a while.'

'We'll see. You didn't get put off, did you? By that stuff about Cyn, and me getting beaten up?'

She shook her head. 'I was surprised though. It sounded as if you went out of your way to find trouble.'

'I did, I suppose.'

'Why?'

'Something to do with the way things were with Cyn and me. Now I want to stay in one piece, all systems go. Mind you, a few hand jobs wouldn't be so bad.'

'Did you do it that way with Cyn?'

It was the first time she'd ever asked me about my sexual past. I hadn't asked much about her and Michael either, but, from what I'd heard of him, it sounded as if he'd hardly have the time. 'No,' I said.

'What about with Ailsa?'

I'd told her a bit about Ailsa. I could hardly avoid it; there were things she'd given me lying around the house. 'No', I said. 'Not with Ailsa either. Look, where's this heading? What's wrong?'

'Oh, I don't know. I just feel shitty. You getting all banged up like this. And the flats . . .'

This seemed like safer ground. 'How's that going?'

She didn't answer for a while. She stared out at the expensive view and I had to scratch her palm to bring her round. 'Hey,' I said.

'Sorry. Well, I found one I like.'

'Good. Where is it?'

'Bondi.'

'Bondi!'

'Tamarama, actually.'

'Jesus, Helen, that's miles away.'

'I really like it. It has this big balcony and a view of the water.'

I felt depressed; I'd envisaged her across the street or over the back fence, not half an hour away. 'What sort of a place? Units or what?'

'It's a big block. Eighty flats. It looks like one of those places along the coast in Spain, but not as flash. You know?'

'No.'

'I knew you'd be against it.'

'All those joints have concrete cancer, did you know?'

'What?'

'They were built with crummy concrete back in the sixties. That'd be about the vintage wouldn't it?'

'Yes.' Our hands had moved apart now and her

110

face was setting into hard lines. Impatience was here with hostility just over the hill, but I couldn't stop myself.

I said, 'I've heard about these places. They're all going to fall down in ten years unless . . .'

'Unless what?'

'Unless everyone in them kicks in lots of dough and has the job fixed.'

She'd turned her head away and was examining the view again. 'It was cheap,' she said softly. 'I thought it was cheap.'

I felt crummy of course. My eye was aching and my throat was dry. I was hungry and thirsty; the sexual feeling had gone, leaving us washed up on separate beaches.

'I'm sorry, love. I could be wrong.'

She stood up. 'Yep, you might be. I'll check it out on Monday. Well, I'd better be off. Dr Stivens'll be here soon.'

'Mister Stivens.'

'You're the expert.' She bent and kissed my cheek; the touch thrilled me and I wanted to unsay everything. Shit, why couldn't *I* move to Bondi? What was sacred about Glebe? 'Helen, I could . . .'

'Bye, Cliff. I'll come and get you at ten tomorrow.'

'We'll go and look at your flat.'

She smiled from the door. 'Have a nice suture adjustment. Bye.'

Stivens arrived with light and mirrors and surgical gloves. He took off the patch, put drops in my eye and fiddled for a few minutes. I didn't feel a thing.

'Good,' he said. 'Not everyone can take that.'

'I couldn't say I enjoyed it. What's the outlook? Sorry, I can't seem to stop saying things about looking.'

'It's a common response. The prognosis is very good. Look after yourself . . .'

'You're doing it too.'

He smiled. 'Take care. Use these drops I'm going to give you as often as you like. When you need them. Keep it covered at night and try not to lie on it. I'd like to see you in a week.'

'No lasting damage then?'

'You were lucky.' He packed his bag. 'You said some strange things under the anaesthetic, Mr Hardy.'

'Like what?'

'You talked about Bermagui. Lovely spot, I've got a small place there I get down to now and then. Have you got a place on the coast?'

I shook my head which hurt a lot. I winced.

'You'll have to watch that. No violent movements for a couple of weeks.'

'Sex?'

'Gently does it.'

'Sometimes,' I said. 'Well, thank you. All I have to do now is pay for it all.'

He busied himself with his bag; they never like to discuss the sordid side. 'You have medical insurance surely, in your profession?'

'No.'

'Most unwise. Well, I suppose you sustained the injury in the line of duty. Your employer could be liable.'

'Maybe. Thank you, Mr Stivens.'

'Call my rooms on Monday for an appointment.'

'See you in Macquarie Street.'

'Good evening, Mr Hardy.'

That, of course, left me with thoughts of Carmel and Leo Wise and the case I'd had with all the threads. Suddenly, most of the threads had been pulled and they'd led nowhere. It was hard to accept that the Agnew-Bourke trail was a red herring but there it was. I tried to think about what remained of the case but the effort made my eye throb.

Stivens had left some pain-killers and I took them

112

with water. I wanted something stronger but there was no prospect of that. Helen had brought some books—Elmore Leonard's *La Brava* and something by Clive James. I started on the Leonard and got interested but it was hard work reading with one eye. It watered, I swore and put the book down. I rang for the nurse and she told me that I'd missed the evening meal which had been served while Stivens was at work. I swore again.

'Don't speak like that to me. It's not my fault.'

'I hear you've got a strong union now?'

'Yes.'

'Good. I bet you're guaranteed your evening meal.'

'I can bring you a cup of tea and a snack at nine.'

'Coffee,' I said. 'Please.'

I was asleep long before it came.

15

HELEN drove me home in her Holden Gemini which was better sprung than the Falcon but harder to get in and out of. She was solicitous but quiet. I got comfortable on the couch in the front room—books, the Saturday papers I'd missed, my pills and eyedrops, wine and TV—all to hand. We ate a salad for lunch; some wine and pain-killers made me feel woozy.

'I'm going over to Bondi,' Helen said. 'Talk to some of the people in the flats, see what goes on.'

'I'll come with you.'

She shook her head. 'You'd be asleep by the end of Glebe Point Road. Take it easy, I won't be long. There was a message from Mr Wise on the machine. Want to hear it?'

'Sure.'

She moved the phone and the recorder closer to me and jiggled her keys. 'Don't get up, will you?'

'Only for nature.'

She kissed me on my stubbled cheek. 'I'd like to hear about this case when I get back. I'm interested, Cliff.'

'Okay. Hope the flat's good. What I was going to say when you left yesterday was that maybe I could move. I don't have to live in Glebe.'

She smiled; when Helen smiles she looks even smarter than when she's not smiling. 'That's something to think about. Okay. See you.'

I played the message tape of Leo Wise's firm but

114

troubled voice. 'Leo Wise, Hardy. I heard you got hurt. I hope it's nothing serious. If it's to do with Carmel I'll be happy to pay the bills and so on. But I'd like to hear developments. This is my weekend number. Call anytime, ah . . . as soon as you're up to it.' He gave the number and hung up. I called it and he came on the line immediately.

'Hardy. Good. You all right?'

'So-so. I've had an eye operation, nothing too serious but I'll have to go quiet for a few days, week maybe.'

'Sorry to hear it. How did it happen? I mean was it . . .?'

'It was sort of related to your daughter's death, sort of.' I told him about the Bourke-Agnew red herring. He listened and didn't interrupt.

'Are you sure this Williamson was telling the truth?'

'Hard to be sure. But I'd say so, yes.'

I heard his sigh. 'Well, I thought it might be something like that. You know, Carmel just in the wrong place at the wrong time.'

'Yeah, I'm sorry, but it doesn't look that way. Of course I'm going to run a few checks on Williamson, but my instinct tells me he's straight. How's your wife?'

'Just fair. So, have you got any other leads?'

'Only one. I'll get on it as soon as I can. Later in the week. Oh, I saw Carmel's film. I thought it was great.'

'Yes. I watched it myself the other night. A mistake that was. Moira cried.'

'I'm sorry. Do you know anything about this documentary she was working on—ah, the lives of the rich, or something?'

'Not really. She was always on about that. How the rich take the bread out of the mouths of the poor.'

115

'Did you fight about it?'

'No. She was very smart, Carmel. She said she had selected her targets and I wasn't one.'

'Targets?'

'Figure of speech. No, we didn't fight.' There was a long pause, so long I felt uncomfortable as you do when you wait for a stammerer to get the words out. 'I think we had the same sort of sense of humour,' he said. 'We didn't fight.'

'Okay, Mr Wise,' I said. 'I'll get back to you as soon as I can.'

Good about the medical bills, I thought. Not so good about the wife. I wanted badly to help Wise but I wasn't optimistic. I had a short sleep, eased the patch off and used the drops in the eye which was gritty and sore, and I drank some wine. Helen had left *Bermagui* in the VCR. I hit the play button and watched the movie again. That's how good it was—good enough to watch twice in 48 hours. I didn't cry like Moira Wise but I was feeling melancholy and uncertain when Helen got back.

'Whatcha been doing?'

'I watched *Bermagui* again.'

'Shit! I was going to do that tonight.'

'I think I could see it again. How's it look at Tamarama?'

'You really want to know?' She poured some wine into a coffee cup for herself and some more into my glass. She swilled it down. 'Phew. That's good. I've been talking non-stop and tramping up and down stairs.'

'Sounds like my job.'

We laughed and she reached over and kissed me. 'Poor you. It was hell. And the results were a bit uncertain.'

'Yup,' I said. 'That's the way it is.'

'Mm. There's a building down the road that has what you said. Concrete cancer. Definitely. And this one, mine, was built by the same mob.'

116

'Oh,' I said.

'But not everyone agrees that mine has the problem. Doesn't look the same. The other one's buggered, mine just looks ... worn.'

I drank some wine and thought about it. 'Still looks good, the view and all?'

'Terrific. Yes.'

'You talked to people in the building and some say it's okay and some say it ain't?'

'That's right.'

'You need to break them down, find out if it's owners that say it's fine and tenants that gripe, or what.'

'That's smart.'

I coughed. 'Training and ... experience.'

'D'you think it'd be wise for me to look at the minutes of the meetings of the corporate body?'

I coughed again. 'Oh, yes, sure.'

'I'm doing that on Monday ...'

'Uh huh.'

'... and getting a professional inspection.'

'I hope they say it'll stand for a thousand years.'

'I'll make us some dinner. Then you can tell me about this Wise case.'

I told her, from the beginning. She listened, smoked her Gitane with coffee after we'd eaten and looked at all the paraphernalia from flat one in the Greenwich Apartments, which I could now mail to the Federal police or throw away.

'How old is she?' she said.

'Who?'

'The mother.'

'I don't know. Carmel was 21. Wise says she's not old, late thirties maybe.'

'He's right. That's not too old to have a child. Did you know that it's often the age of the male that's the factor in having defective kids?'

'No.'

'That's true. It doesn't get much in the way of press space as a scientific fact, but it's true.'

'Yes. Well, Wise seems willing to risk it if his wife can get over this.'

'You've watched the film twice. Are there any clues in that?'

'Not really. I was interested in what her father said—about her having targets.'

'The flatmate might be able to tell you more about that.'

'And this Jan de Vries.'

'Have you got anything else?'

'Not much. The producer of the TV documentary said she might have been too good for the job, too classy, something like that. I'd like to know what he meant.'

'You think the answer lies in her filmmaking?'

'She doesn't seem to have done anything else.'

'She *must* have. You'll find something. Will he wait?'

'What d'you mean?'

'Wise. You're not going to be able to do anything for a couple of weeks.'

'I'd go crazy doing nothing for a couple of weeks.'

'Cliff. Don't be an idiot.'

'Nobody said nothin' about doin' nothin'. Oh, except Stivens said gently does it when it comes to sex.'

'You asked him?'

'Of course.'

'Gently does it?'

'That's right.'

'Does it?'

'Let's see if it does.'

She helped me up the stairs, she helped me into bed, she helped all down the line. Afterwards, I lay beside her and listened to her gentle breathing as she slept. I fancied I could hear surf beating on a

118

beach and the cries of seagulls. I thought I could live by the beach or I could live in the mountains. I could live anywhere within striking distance of the city if I had to. And I would, to have her sleeping beside me at night. Some nights.

16

IT was over the next couple of days that Helen started to call me what Whitlam had called McMahon, 'the Tiberius of the telephone'. I made use of the sorts of contacts you build up in this business, to check on Williamson and Rolf. Establishing that they were Federal cops took a while, and finding that, within the usual limits of narcotics law enforcement, they were honest, took even longer.

Carmel Wise's flatmate, Judy Syme, remembered me and listened while I described Williamson, Rolf and the other man I'd seen at Shetland Island. My question was, could they have been the men who came to Studio Eight in Randwick before Carmel Wise died.

'No,' she said. 'Positively not. They didn't look at all like that, none of them.'

'Have you thought of anything else that might be useful, since we talked?'

'No. Oh, one thing. They took a couple of copies of the movie.'

'Carmel's movie?'

'Yes. That one I lent you. It was put away somewhere. They took the ones that were lying around.'

'Did they say anything about it?'

'I don't think so. 'Course, I was so frightened I mightn't have noticed.'

'Did Carmel ever say anything to you about targets? About having people as targets?'

'N . . . no, I did hear her use the word on the phone one time.'

'Who was she talking to?'

'Jan de Vries.'

But there I hit a wall. I phoned the Film & Television School and was told that Dr de Vries had not been in for a couple of days and no, that wasn't unusual. They wouldn't give me his address or private phone number. I left a message for him—my name and number, my line of work and that it had to do with Carmel Wise. I then got de Vries' number from Judy Syme. He lived in Lane Cove, close to his work but a long way from the GPO. There I was again, thinking the Inner West was the only place to live. I called the number and got a woman, impatient, upset or crazy.

'Yes? Yes? What do you want?'

'I'd like to speak to Dr de Vries, please.'

'Not here!' She hung up vigorously, or miserably or madly.

My next call was to the producer of the documentary Carmel Wise had worked on. Tim Edwards was one of the principals of Paladin Pictures Inc. He sounded young and keen, eager to talk in a rapid-fire style about filmmaking, and a bit green. In my limited experience old hands in that business don't say that someone has 'too much flair'; old hands don't really say anything that has any meaning.

'Leo Wise? Sure I know him. I got Carmel to introduce us once. Thought he might back a project, him being a rich business man and all.'

'Did he?'

'Wasn't long before Carmel died. Seemed interested at the time. He might have. Nice guy. How can I help you, Mr Hardy?'

'You're quoted as saying that Carmel might have too much flair for the project. What did that mean?'

'It means, oops.'

'Come again.'

'I shouldn't have said that.'

'You did say it though and it could be important

to me. What's the documentary about, exactly.'

'I've still got funding hassles with it and distribution problems. I can't ...'

'I'm not in the business. I won't tell a soul. It could be important. Did she overstep the mark somehow?'

'Yeah. It wasn't meant to be a revolutionary number, you understand? Not pap but not barricades stuff. We got the permission of these ten ... well eight actually, that's one of the hassles I've got ... of these rich people to film them and do a few interviews.'

'Sounds like something between *Sixty Minutes* and that thing about the movie stars ...'

'*Life Styles of the Rich and Famous*, well, yeah, maybe. Carmel, she wouldn't leave it alone. Kept trying to get footage they didn't want taken. She tried to change the scripts, even stuck herself into one interview. Terrific filmmaker, brilliant editor, but lousy judgement. She really hurt me, although she did a wonderful job on editing the footage I can use.'

'I don't quite follow. Did two of the subjects pull out?'

'You got it.'

'Sort of as a reaction to what Carmel did?'

'Yeah.'

'Who were they?'

'Why?'

'Come on, the girl's dead, and no-one knows why.'

'I thought she got caught up in the porno rackets.'

'Do you really believe that?'

'I'd like to see a porn movie made by Carmel. It'd sizzle.'

'Forget it. She didn't make any. Who pulled out?'

'Bastards, why should I care? Marjorie Legge and Phillip Broadhead.'

'Do you have any of the stuff you shot on them?'

'No. I had to give it up. Broadhead threatened to contact the others and get the plug pulled on the whole thing if I didn't surrender the film. I'm in debt over it. I had no choice.'

'How did Carmel react?'

'Angrily. Look, if that's all, I've got work to do.'

I thanked him, hung up and looked at the two names I had on my pad. Marjorie Legge had a chain of high fashion boutiques. She appeared on television shows and ghost-written articles signed by her were published in the papers. She had been profitably married several times and her views were extremely right wing. A story was told about her that on a talk-back radio show she had advised an old-age pensioner, calling in to complain of boredom and financial hardship, to take up French cooking.

She was a scourge of the feminists and one of their chief targets. *Targets! Well, well*, I thought, there was an interesting word. Maybe I should take up free associating as an analytical technique.

Marjorie Legge was currently married to a man whose name I couldn't recall but who was reputed to be a very heavy number. With those connections, Marjorie Legge could be a very dangerous person to offend.

Phillip Broadhead was known as 'Mr Racing'. He gave his occupation to the various committees of inquiry that investigated him over the years as 'commission agent'. No-one knew what that was, but everyone knew what Phil did, which was more or less what Phil had always done. He was the finance behind several leading on-course bookmakers, and also the money and the muscle and whatever else was required, behind Sydney's major SP operation. Phil had gone to one of the pricier Sydney private schools (where he had probably run the book on the GPS Head of the River). He knew policemen and politicians and trade union bosses and media mag-

123

nates and everyone else it was useful to know. He had one conviction, back in the forties, for assaulting his then wife.

Phillip Broadhead had been investigated and written up in the tabloids so many times that all this was on the public record. There were many entries on him in the indexes to the recent spate of books about organised crime in Sydney. The sorts of books journalists write when they get hold of one hard piece of information, and embellish it with a lot of speculation and off-the-record stuff. Phil was good embellishment but his police record was the best pointer to the amount of protection he had. The mind boggled at the thought of fearless, freelance Carmel Wise sniffing around him.

All this phoning and cross-referencing took a couple of days. It was interspersed with pill-taking, eyedrops and long sleeps. The house brick effect hadn't developed, but the right eye was sore all the time and the other got tired from over-use. It was hard to read, hard to watch television, hard to sit still. It was also hard to follow developments regarding Helen's flat. The more I thought about Phil Broadhead's mansion at Huntley Point and Jan de Vries' unhappy-sounding home at Lane Cove, the more I wanted to stay in Glebe.

'The loan looks okay,' Helen told me on my third night home.

'Oh, good. Can you apply that to any place you find, or is it tied to . . . ?'

'Go on, say it. I know you'll have some smart name for the place.'

'The cancer ward.'

She laughed. 'Shit, Cliff. No, it's good for a couple of months. Any place that passes inspection.'

'And how's that going?'

'Still waiting.'

'Still looking?'

'No. I know I should be.' She poured some coffee and held up the pills inquiringly. When I shook my head she went on. 'How many houses have you owned?'

'Just this one. Me and the bank.'

'I've had a couple. It's always the same. Once you get interested in a place you start imagining yourself there—shopping, parking, making changes, you know.'

'Mm.'

'I shouldn't be doing it with this joint. Not if it's going to fall through.'

'Fall through,' I said. 'Interesting choice of phrase.'

'Stop it, Cliff.'

'Sorry. When will you hear?'

'Tomorrow, I hope.'

'Shouldn't there be lots of places going. I mean, with the tax changes? Aren't people getting out of property as an investment? I read something about it. They've got to sell before a certain time to avoid the taxes. It should be a buyer's market.'

'I like this place.'

'Yeah. Well, tomorrow.'

'What're you going to do? More phoning?'

'No, I'm finished phoning.' I told her about Marjorie Legge and 'Mr Racing' and the other new threads I had to pull.

'So, what next?'

'Action.'

'Cliff, you can't . . .'

'Gentle action. I'm going to the police.'

'You're what?'

'I need them.'

'You always say you *don't* need them, apart from Frank Parker. You don't need the leaks and the paperwork and the lack of imagination.'

'I just need them for tomorrow.'

125

17

I phoned Mercer the next morning before putting through a call to Drew. They call it chain of command or some such thing—I think it's so they can keep an eye on each other. Drew wasn't happy about it, but he agreed to let me come to the police building to investigate the evidence they were holding in the Carmel Wise case.

'You want to see the car or what?' Drew managed to keep the hostility under check, just.

'I want to see the bag.'

'What bag?'

'The bag that the cassettes were in.'

'Why?'

'Maybe it isn't her bag.'

He laughed. 'You won't get anywhere with that, Hardy.'

'Why not?'

'It isn't anybody's bag, or it could be anybody's. It's a supermarket shopping bag, plastic, not new, smeared with prints.'

'I want to see the videos then.'

I could see the leer on his face. 'No, can't allow that. No facilities here for that.'

'I just want to look at the stuff, I mean, examine it physically, not experience it emotionally.'

'Huh?'

'I just want to look, not play.'

'College Street annexe. Make it 11.30. I'll give you fifteen minutes.'

I was getting around the house on my own by this time—showering and dressing, managing the stairs, but the great big outside world was another matter. I almost went headfirst into the gutter trying to get into the taxi, and I bumped my head when I got out. The restricted vision made me slow and tentative on the city footpaths, and hesitant about crossing the roads. Still, it was good to be a part of functioning humanity again.

I copped my first handicapped person joke from Bill Moore, the receptionist at the police building, an old warrior out to graze whom I knew slightly. 'Well, what d'you know?' he said. 'Private eye is right, just the one, eh, Cliff?'

'Shit, Bill,' I said, 'it's supposed to be a disguise and you penetrated it right off. I'm here to see Detective Constable Drew, in the annexe he said.'

'Lucky you. Hold on.' He lifted a phone and spoke briefly into it. 'Okay. I should search you for concealed weapons but if you had one and it was concealed you'd have trouble finding it with one eye, wouldn't you.'

'I don't know.' I mimed shooting with two fingers. 'I close this eye anyway, when I shoot.'

'Through there, Cliff. Look after yourself.'

I went down some steps, using the handrail, and through a set of heavy glass doors. The place was halfway between a laboratory and a locker room. Scientific equipment was lined up on benches; there were stools and small tables, ropes and pulleys and several well-stocked bookcases. Along one wall was a bank of green lockers. A tall man whose little remaining hair was blonde, sat on a stool near the lockers. He beckoned me over.

'Hardy?'

'Yes.'

'Drew.'

We shook hands. I sensed an immediate dislike of

127

me in him which I was prepared to reciprocate. He had a hard face just beginning to go flabby; the way he sat on the stool and stuck out his hand just far enough, suggested that he expected a lot of things to be done for him and would do bugger all in return.

'You're wasting your time,' he said.

'It's my time.'

'Well, you'd be getting paid for it, wouldn't you?'

'Yeah, I hope so. I'm not a public servant though, I can't count on a pay cheque every month.'

He digested that with difficulty but evidently decided it wasn't worth a response. He put his hand in his jacket pocket and produced a key. For a minute I thought he was going to throw it to me but he didn't.

'Take a look. Fifteen minutes, as I said.'

'That's about what your boys gave the flat.'

'What does that mean?'

'Nothing.' I took the key and looked for the number along the rows of lockers. It was hard with one eye and in the dim light. Eventually I located it high on the fourth level. I had to stand on tiptoe to get the key in the door. I opened the locker and brought a stool across, climbed on it and took out everything inside. Drew sat on his stool ten feet away as I laid the stuff out on a bench.

'What happened to your eye. You get it poked while you were peeping in a window?'

I glanced at him; he was was one of those balding men who look as if they've never had a hair to spare and have suffered with every one lost. Maybe it wasn't his fault, but I wasn't in the mood for his cracks. 'No,' I said. I opened the plastic bag. 'Your wife's naked beauty dazzled me, know what I mean, pal?'

'Don't touch that!' he snarled.

'Stop trying so hard to be the nastiest cop in town, Drew. You've got the title. Why don't you go

128

and have a smoke or something and leave me in peace.'

He'd got off the stool and taken two steps towards me but perhaps even Drew balked at belting a man with one eye. 'I'm staying here and your time's running out.'

'You're a prince.' There wasn't a lot to see. A supermarket shopping bag with eight video cassettes in it. Four more cassettes were tied in a bundle with string, with a tag reading 'Car' attached. There were a few other items which had evidently come from the car—a scarf, a comb and a book—Pauline Kael's *500 Nights at the Movies*.

'What about the things she was carrying? Purse, cigarettes, money?'

'What're you trying to say?'

'Jesus, Drew. What's your middle name, Aggression? I'm only asking.'

He sniffed and wiped his nose. *Are bald men more liable to colds?* I wondered.

'No purse, no cigarettes. Some money in her jeans. A small amount of marijuana, some papers. That's there, in an envelope. The clothes were pretty messed up with blood. The . . . ah, reasonable stuff was turned over to her parents.'

I found the envelope and opened it—enough for two or three joints, Tally Ho papers. The sort of thing anyone under 50 might have around. The cassettes were not quite so standard. Some titles had an Oriental flavour—*Bamboo Babies, Viet Virgins*—and others a military tone—*GI Johns, Marine Studs*. There was no difference in quality and subject between the two lots of cassettes, those in the bag and those from the car, except that the former had some bloodstains on them.

'Tell me about the car.'

'What d'you mean? Hey, keep those things separate!'

'You're going to learn something, Drew, my friend. What condition was the car in?'

'All right, except that one of the doors was sprung. You know these sleazos, they'll drive around with no lights, busted doors . . .'

'Yeah, I'll bet yours is immaculate. Well, you can forget about the porn angle.'

'What the hell're you talking about?'

I held up the cassettes. 'You see these? They're Beta, right? All the other cassettes in the flats are VHS. Did you know the girl made a film? I've seen it on a VHS cassette. VHS in the flat, VHS where she lived. This crap was planted, Drew. It was dropped by the body and put in the car. You need a new angle.'

It rocked him. 'Jesus, I told Mercer we had it . . .'

'Unforgiving type, Mercer.'

The effort to treat me as a human being almost gave him a hernia. 'Look, Hardy, have you got anything? I mean . . .'

I grinned at him. Grinning hurt the sore eye but it was worth it. 'Why don't you put all this stuff away, Drew? Many thanks for the help. If you can be of any further assistance I'll let you know.'

18

MY eye ached. I went to a pub and treated it in the
toilet—peeled off the patch, used the eyedrops and replaced the pad—then I had a glass of wine and a sand-
wich. Chewing hurt; I took a couple of pain-killers and
felt better, almost cheerful. Using a phone in the bar,
I rang Leo Wise and confirmed his opinion that
Carmel had no connection with the pornographic
videos.

'Thanks, Hardy. Are those cops dumb, or could
they be in on it somehow?'

'The one I spoke to seemed genuinely surprised.
Doesn't rule out others of course, but my guess is
they're not involved. Did Carmel ever talk to you
about Marjorie Legge?'

'No.'

Maybe it was the noise in the bar, maybe just
discretion, but I dropped my voice and moved the
mouthpiece closer. 'Phil Broadhead?'

'No, I don't think so. Or just as anyone might. As a
character, you know. What do they have to do with
it?'

'Maybe nothing. I'm looking into it. What about
Jan de Vries?'

'I've heard the name. Who's she?'

'He. He's a lecturer at the film school, seems he and
Carmel were close.'

'I knew there was someone around she spent time
with. But I thought it was to do with work. Are you
saying it was something else?'

'Yes. Would her mother know anything?'

'She might. Yes, she might.'

'Would it be all right for me to talk to her? I don't want to upset her.'

'That'd be okay, I think. When?'

'Well, maybe tonight. It might not be necessary if other things pan out. But it could be tonight.'

'Okay. You know where we are.'

'Thanks.'

'How's the eye?'

'Not bad.'

I left the pub and walked out into bright afternoon sunlight. I put on dark glasses, which sat awkwardly over the patched eye, and tried to flag down a cab. I couldn't see the signs properly and I waved at full ones and let empty ones go by. Eventually one pulled in. I lowered myself carefully into the front seat and gave him the Lane Cove address. He shoved the Gregory's at me and lit a cigarette.

'Look it up for me, will you? I don't know that area too well.'

'Mate,' I said, 'with this eye I can hardly read the meter. Why don't you get on the road and pull over somewhere in the vicinity and check the address? And put the cigarette out, please. The smoke hurts my eye.'

'Sorry, sir.' He was young and only practising at being tough.

To be perfect, Lane Cove should look different in autumn. There should be a carpet of russet leaves on the ground and the trees should be all soft reds and yellows. It isn't like that, but it looks as if it should be. The front gardens in de Vries' street were deep and wide and the side fences seemed designed not to spoil the afforested look.

'Nice street,' the driver said. I'd been quiet on the drive and it seemed to make him nervous. 'You live here?'

'No. Visiting.'

'How long you going to be?'

'About an hour.'

'Where to then?'

'Glebe, I guess. Why? I don't fancy holding you here with the meter running.'

'No, no. I need a break. I could take it now and be back in an hour. It'd suit me.'

'Okay.' I paid him and gave him a reasonable tip, or Leo Wise did. He thanked me and came around to help me out of the car. He was dark, short and strongly built, around twenty years of age and trying to be friendly. I noticed he had a slim, battered paperback sticking out of the hip pocket of his jeans. 'Thanks. What're you reading?'

'Dostoevsky, *The Gambler*. You read it?'

'Long time ago. I read a couple of his short ones.'

He grinned. 'Me too. Okay, sir, I'll see you in an hour.'

De Vries' house was a wide timber construction, painted white, and well cared for. The garden featured the appropriate big, but not too big, trees along with some shrubs and a deep mat of ivy as ground cover. It was a pleasant, cool, shady garden in front of a pleasant-looking house. The only thing that wouldn't be good about it would be the mortgage payments.

I walked up to the front porch and rang the bell. The woman who answered it was big and fair with pale eyes and lips. She wore a shapeless white dress which badly needed washing and sandals with incongruously high heels.

'Yes?' She leaned against the doorway and her eye level was nearly the same as mine.

'Mrs de Vries?'

'Yes, I suppose. Who are you?' She had an accent, somewhere between American and South African, which I hadn't detected on the phone.

'My name is Hardy. I rang you a day or so back. I

133

need, very urgently, to talk to your husband.'

'You need . . . very urgently,' she mocked. 'So do I.'

'I don't understand.' She started to close the door and I shuffled closer; maybe I put my patched eye where the shut door would go because she stopped the movement.

'Go away,' she said.

'Where's Jan de Vries?'

'Gone. Left. What do you care? What does anyone care?'

'When?'

'See? Who cares? When? Why d'you want to know when?'

'It's important.'

'To you. Two weeks ago. I haven't heard from him in two weeks. Now, would you please go away!'

'Mrs de Vries, have you ever heard of a woman named Carmel Wise?'

She pushed back some of the tumbling fair hair and looked hard at me. Some colour came into her pallid face. 'Yes, I've heard of her. Jan's lover, she is.'

'This is important, Mrs de Vries. Could I come in? I think we need to talk.'

'I haven't talked to anyone for two weeks. Only the children. Are you a policeman?'

'Not exactly.' I showed her my licence. She examined it and then my face. For a woman of her size, a man with a surgical eye patch can't be too frightening. She stood aside.

'Come in.'

The passage was a sea of newspapers, magazines and children's toys and books. We picked our way over and through it and went into a living room where a party had been held. There was a glass on every level surface, bottles, cans, overflowing ashtrays, paper plates with food clinging to them and the sickly sweet smell of stale, trapped, over-

134

used air. She flopped into a chair, just missing a paper plate with cheese dip on it.

'We had a party. At the end of the party Jan told me he was leaving me. And he left. I haven't ...' She waved her hand at the room.

'I thought you had children?'

'Two. They are staying with friends.'

'So should you.'

She shrugged; her big, loose breasts moved under the stained white dress. 'I have no friends here.'

I looked around, stalling for time and wondering how to handle it. The room was big, the windows were big, the carpet was deep and through a door I could see a sunny sitting room with a polished floor. A load of washing had been dumped in the middle of the floor. It was an upper income house and should have been filled with sounds like Mozart on the hi-fi and the buzz of the home computer; instead it felt like an army barracks after the regiment has pulled out.

'Mrs de Vries ...'

'Barbara.' I was sure now the accent was American. 'Well, Mr Detective, what do you want with my husband?'

There was a slightly mad air about her, as if she'd built a sort of crazy shelter for herself. She kept tumbling and untumbling her hair. She was tilting but she hadn't fallen; I thought she could take some direct talking. 'Carmel Wise is dead. She was shot.'

The hair flew everywhere and her hands slapped hard against her cheeks. 'Oh, my god! Jan ...?'

'No. Not by him and he ... he's alive as far as I know.' The words pushed ideas around in my brain. *Why not de Vries? Because of the bag of Beta tapes. Why is he hiding? Because he knows what killed Carmel?*

'What happened to Carmel?'

'You knew her?'

135

'Oh, sure. Jan brought her here. I could see what was going on. She wasn't the first and not the worst either . . . ' She broke off and started gnawing at a knuckle. I told her the story in outline. She interrupted a few times and we established that the party had been held two nights before Carmel was killed. Barbara de Vries hadn't read the papers or watched TV in that time and she hadn't done much since. When I'd finished, the knuckle was red raw. She nodded sympathetically a few times but when she spoke it was all direct self-interest. 'If she is dead, perhaps he will come back to me.'

'Would you accept that?'

'Of course. We Pennsylvania Dutch women will accept anything.'

'Could you tell me a little about yourself and your husband? I'd like a photograph of him if you have one.'

She stood and tottered out of the room. When she came back she handed me a colour snapshot. It showed a stocky man with a drooping moustache and dark hair hanging over his forehead. He looked about as Dutch as Michael Spinks.

'He doesn't look Dutch,' I said.

'Yes, that's right. But he is and I'm not.'

'But you said . . . '

'Pennsylvania Dutch. That's what we're called at home. But I'm German by descent. Jan's people were Dutch but he is a 100 per cent American.' She said it with an ironic smile. There was more colour in her face and lips now and she looked as if she could be a good-looking woman in better circumstances.

'Forgive me for being blunt, but what's he doing here, then?'

Again the smile. 'A job. There are not so many jobs for 100 per cent Americans anymore.'

She told me that Jan de Vries was a graduate in film from somewhere and a PhD from UCLA. They had met when he was attempting to run a small, independent film distribution company. He had hired her as a secretary and things had gone on from there. The company failed and Australia offered the best job prospects.

'Jan is a radical,' she said. 'We came here in 1975.'

'Not such a good year for a radical,' I said.

'Not at the end, no. Jan was furious about it.'

'How does he feel about now?'

'More furious still.'

'What about you?'

'I was a secretary, then I was a wife, now I am a mother. That is the trouble. Oh,' she tumbled the hair again, 'it is good to talk. Thank you. I feel better. Would you like some tea? The kitchen is a mess too, but I could ...'

'No, thank you. I have to go.' My hour was almost up. 'You have no idea where your husband is?'

She shook her head. 'I don't know where they went to do it.'

'When did you last hear from him?'

'On the morning after he left. He telephoned to ask if the children were all right.'

I was checking through my mental list, the one that covers what people do when they flit. 'Did he take his passport, Mrs de Vries?'

The idea was a new one, but she shook her head quickly. 'No. I saw it just now when I got the photograph.'

'How did he sound on the telephone?'

She considered it as if for the first time. 'I was so mad. I never thought he would leave me.'

'He said he was leaving to live with Carmel?'

'Live? I don't know. Live? I am not sure.'

'What, then?'

'He spent all the time at the party with her. Then he said he had to go with her. Something like that. I had drunk a lot. We fought. He said he had to go.

137

Go, I said. Go!' She was crying now but she stifled it and wiped her face with her hands. 'I must pull myself together.'

'I'm sorry. How did he sound on the phone?'

'He sounded frightened.'

'Frightened of what?'

She shook her head. I asked her if she wanted me to send someone over to help her but she refused. She said again, as if she liked the phrase, that she'd pull herself together. I thought she could do it. She said I could keep the photograph; I gave her a card and the usual spiel about calling me if anything happened or if she wanted help. She thanked me a couple of times. Before she let me out she kicked off her sandals; I expect she rolled up her sleeves as soon as the door was closed.

The taxi was waiting. I sniffed at the kid a bit for alcohol as I got in but all I smelled was tobacco. 'Glebe, you said?'

'Right.' I gave him the address and settled back to think about what I'd learned from Barbara de Vries. Suddenly I got a stabbing pain in the eye and I gasped.

'Hey, you all right?'

'Yeah. Just the eye. I need to put some drops in it. Could you stop a minute?'

He pulled over and I got to work on the patch. He turned off the meter and helped me by holding the bottle of drops and producing a tissue. 'How'd it happen?'

'I was running away from some people who didn't mean me any harm as it turned out. Thanks. That's good.'

'What line of work are you in?'

I told him.

'Yeah?' He fumbled for a cigarette, remembered and stopped. 'That's tremendous!'

'Let's get going. It's not really tremendous. It's

mostly like what you've just seen me do—visit people.'

'I see the gun too.'

I grunted. 'I haven't used one in a long time. How's the Dostoevsky going?'

He flicked the meter on, started up, checked the traffic and pulled out in a series of smooth, easy movements. 'Finished it. Great! How d'you get into your business?'

'By bad luck. What're your plans? Taxi driving must interfere with your reading.'

He laughed. 'Yeah, it does. Everything does. Oh, I dunno. I've done a few things. Ran a lawn-mowing business for a while. Lotta work, not much dough. I sold it. I've got an interest in the cab. Not much but it's better than nothing.' He put his right hand across his body. 'Scott Galvani's the name.'

'Cliff Hardy,' I said. We shook quickly. 'You're kidding—Scott Galvani?'

'No, dinkum. My parents, they're Sicilian, but I was born here. They reckoned Scott was a true-blue Aussie name.' He laughed. 'Maybe they were right.'

'Maybe.' I glanced into the back seat and saw several paperbacks in a half beer carton. 'You buy them in job lots? the books?'

'Sort of. I carry a few around, never know what I'm going to read next. Think I might try Gunter Grass. What d'you reckon?'

'Out of my depth,' I said. 'You turn here. You know Glebe?'

'Sure. I live in Leichhardt. Look, Cliff, what case're you working on now?'

'I told you, it isn't like on TV.'

'Still. You have to get around, right?'

'Yes.'

'And you can't drive?'

'Not for a while.'

'You need an assistant.'

'No.'

'Come on. A driver, call it.'

'Why would you want to do that?'

He scratched his dark, whiskered chin. 'Call it work experience. I'm thinking of going into the security business.'

'It's overstocked.'

'I'm multi-lingual. English, French, Italian ... well, Sicilian.'

'What else?'

'I'm a wrestler. Would you believe it? I'm a top-notch wrestler and you know how much money there is in wrestling?'

'How much?'

'Zilch. Come on. Cliff. You've gotta go out again tonight, right?'

'Why d'you say that ... Scott?'

'You didn't look happy coming out of that house. You looked thoughtful. Like you said, you visit people. I bet you've got someone to visit tonight.'

He pulled the cab up outside the house. The Falcon sat where Rolf had parked it. Helen's Gemini was behind it. I was tired and hungry and thirsty. I needed a rest and a drink and some time to think. And I had to go and see Mrs Wise. 'Okay,' I said. 'When can you knock off?'

'Now. Let me help you in and I can meet the Missus.'

'I haven't got a Missus.'

'Who's this at the door then?'

Helen came to the gate. She was looking spectacularly good in a red shirt and jeans. Scott Galvani broke the taxi driver's record for getting out and assisting a passenger—not the world's hardest record to break. He helped me to the gate.

'You look terrible,' Helen said.

'I'll be right. Helen Broadway, this is Scott Galvani.'

140

'Hi' Galvani said.

'Hello. Are you going to pay the fare, Cliff?'

'Hey, hey, don't worry about it,' Galvani lit the cigarette he'd been waiting for.

'What?' Helen said. 'Free rides?'

'I've got to go out again later, love. Scott's going to drive me. Might need a bit of help.'

'You can't afford a driver.'

'Hey, I'll work for free.'

'You must be good,' Helen said.

19

SCOTT Galvani came into the house. Before we knew it, he was cooking spaghetti bolognaise, scooting down to the bottle shop for a flagon of red, and generally being entertaining and helpful. He let Helen try out her Italian on him and he praised her efforts.

'Six months there, really workin' at it, you'd be like a native.'

'What I wouldn't give,' Helen said.

This is getting out of hand, I thought. Bondi is one thing, Palermo is another.

The spaghetti was terrific. Galvani washed the dishes and didn't sing in the kitchen.

'He's nice,' Helen said.

'He's persistent.'

Over coffee I talked about the Wise case and Galvani nodded.

'I read about it. The video girl.'

'That's crap! There's something else behind it. Marjorie Legge or Phil Broadhead or someone like that.'

Galvani whistled. 'That's heavy.'

'It could be. I'll back off fast if it is, don't worry.'

Helen glanced at me. Galvani was smoking filter tips and she had just lit her Gitane. The smoke was hurting my eye but I didn't want to spoil her pleasure. I grinned at her but Galvani frowned. 'I don't get you, man.'

'I just want something to satisfy her father. I'm not out to clean up Sydney.'

'Oh, right,' he said.

I drank coffee and thought about what I had to work with. It wasn't much. Essentially I had to find Jan de Vries and find out why he was frightened.

'Why is he frightened?' Helen said.

'Who?'

'Jan de Vries.'

'Are you a mind-reader now?'

'It's the obvious question.'

'Yeah,' Galvani said.

'Look, Scott, I'm not sure this is such a good idea, you tagging along. I *might* get a line on de Vries to-night from the mother.'

'Hope so,' he said.

'I haven't got any worker's compensation policy or anything like that.'

'I'll sign a waiver.'

'Did you read that or see it on TV?'

'What's the difference? When do we go?'

Galvani went to the toilet and Helen put on a jacket. 'Think I'll go over to Ruth's,' she said. She kissed me and I could taste the French tobacco and Australian wine. 'You're an idiot to go out with an eye like that but I know I can't stop you. Tell you what, though, I'm glad you've got him along.'

Something bothered me on the drive to Leo Wise's house in Bellevue Hill. In fact the worry had started back when Scott asked me which car I wanted to take, the Falcon or the taxi.

'The taxi, I think. Nobody looks at a taxi when it's parked.' *But who cares who's looking?* I thought. As I say, it nagged at me as we drove. Scott took it easy out of consideration for my damaged state and he kept the chatter to a minimum. It was a cool night; I had on boots, corduroy pants, a thick shirt and a light jacket. I had the gun under my left arm-pit. What I'd really need, if there was any trouble, would be a cricketer's helmet with visor. Scott had pulled a sweater on over his T-shirt. I could tell that

143

he wanted to smoke but he chewed on a toothpick instead.

'Here it is. Not bad!'

I pointed ahead and he let the taxi roll on past the house. It was big and white, behind a high white wall. Inside the wall there'd be a tennis court and swimming pool. Inside the house there'd be a miserable woman.

'What do I do?' Scott asked.

'I told you it wouldn't be exciting. You wait.'

'Can I put the light on to read?'

'No.'

'What about the radio?'

'Softly.'

'Okay, Cliff. Good luck. You want me to honk if there's any suspicious characters around?'

'No. Run them over.'

There was an intercom by the front gate. I buzzed and got Leo Wise's voice, distorted by the device. 'Yes.'

'Cliff Hardy, Mr Wise. Can I come in?'

'Push the gate,' he said. There was a bleep from somewhere and the gate gave easily. I walked up a flagstoned path, bordered by flowers, to wide steps in front of the house. There was a bright light over the front door but the house was so wide the sides of the building were in shadow. It had two storeys, with a wide balcony supported by wrought iron pillars running across the front and around both sides. Windows from the upper level let out onto the balcony; all those windows in the front were dark.

Leo Wise opened the door before I could knock.

'Evening, Hardy,' he said. 'You look different with the patch. How is it?'

'Evening, Mr Wise. No good for horse riding or swimming, otherwise okay. How's your wife?'

'Composed.' I went into a sort of lobby with a high ceiling but no candelabra. Wise beckoned me towards a set of carved wooden doors off to one side.

144

'Would you like a drink or something, or do you want to see her straight away?'

He opened the doors and we entered a study-cum-library. It was furnished with restraint—comfortable chairs, a writing desk and bookcases. It had cost a lot of money to keep it that modest.

'I'll see her now, if that's all right.'

'Yes it is. Have a seat. I'll get her. I might go off and do a few things on my own if you don't mind. Moira finds me inhibiting sometimes, or so she says.'

'She knows what I'm doing?'

'More or less.'

He went out through another door; I sat down and picked up a magazine. I looked at it without absorbing anything which is how magazines usually affect me.

Moira Wise came into the room and I started absorbing. She was taller than I'd expected, slim and dark-haired. She smiled and the effect of the large, dark eyes and slightly gapped teeth was devastating; she was dimmed by sadness and miles away from beautiful but I felt I could look at her all night. I started to rise but she stopped me.

'Stay there, Mr Hardy. Leo told me about your eye. Getting up must be painful. I'll sit here.' She sat in a chair a few feet away and crossed her legs. She was wearing a black blouse and a white skirt, medium heels on plain black shoes. Once again, money spent on a tasteful, quiet effect. She cocked her head slightly to one side like someone correcting a small squint. 'You're not what I expected.'

'Oh, how's that?'

'I expected someone bulkier, like ... Robert Mitchum.'

'You're a movie fan too, then?'

'Yes, I think Carmel got that from me. What do you want to ask me, Mr Hardy?'

'You know that the police idea, that Carmel was in-

145

volved in a pornographic racket, is bunk?'

'You're too modest. You've shown that. We're grateful. I couldn't see the point when Leo said he was going to hire someone, but something good has come of it. All that video girl rubbish, it was . . . awful.'

Her voice was low-pitched, educated Sydney, without affectation. She didn't seem like a strong woman though, more one who held up well when the going was good and not so well at other times. She was going to be hard to talk to if there was anything she wanted to hide. It felt as if she'd crack if dropped. 'Do you know why Leo wants me to . . . persist, Mrs Wise?'

'Not exactly.'

'I think he wants to have a good memory of Carmel. To understand what happened. To be rid of doubts.'

She smiled. 'Oh, that's Leo all right. He doesn't like doubts.' She drew a deep breath. 'No doubt he's right. Oh, a pun, of sorts.'

I nodded, drew a breath myself, and plunged in. 'I've talked to lots of people who knew Carmel. They all liked her, all thought she was a great artist. I've seen her film and I agree. It was a fine piece of work.'

'Thank you.'

'There was only one person who expressed anything but dismay and loss at Carmel being killed.'

'And who is that?'

'If you and Carmel were close, if you talked together and shared things, I think you know who it would be.'

'Barbara de Vries.'

'That's right, Mrs Wise.'

'What does she have to do with this?'

'Please tell me about Dr de Vries and Carmel, then I'll answer your question. Leo thought Carmel had

146

never had a serious relationship, but this thing with de Vries was serious, wasn't it?'

'Yes. Very.'

'Why didn't Leo know?'

She made fists of her hands and rubbed them together. 'Carmel asked me not to tell him.'

'Why?'

'He was so unsuitable—married, a radical . . .'

'You should see his house in Lane Cove. His lifestyle is about as radical as Marcos'.'

'I see. Still, I couldn't see any future in it for Carmel. Neither could she.'

'What do you mean?'

'They fought all the time. It was on and off, on and off. Carmel used to get very upset.'

'What did they fight about? Did she want him to leave his wife?'

'No, no. Carmel is . . . was . . . was always an unconventional girl. No. They fought about the work they were doing.'

It suddenly seemed warm in the room. There was a slight draught from somewhere lifting the covers of the magazine I'd looked at, but it wasn't enough. I felt hot. I was sure I was getting close to the heart of it. 'What work *were* they doing, Mrs Wise?'

'I'm not really sure. I didn't see Carmel all that often, about once a week, sometimes not.'

'But you talked when you did?'

'Oh, yes. we talked. You'll have seen that we were alike, physically?'

I nodded.

'Emotionally too, I think. We could always understand each other . . . sympathise . . .' She was close to tears now; her head was bent and she was fighting for control. I sat very still and sweated. After a minute she got the control. Her head came up and she was dry-eyed. 'That's why it's so terrible. I miss her so badly, you see. As you might miss a friend.

147

But more than a friend. Do you have any children, Mr Hardy?'

'No.'

'Don't.'

This is a bad break for Leo, I thought. But I didn't want it to turn out like that. This woman deserved better luck. I felt like a blackjack dealer, slipping out the cards. 'I have to know about the work, Mrs Wise. It's important.'

'To whom?'

I went out on a limb. 'Don't you think Carmel would want you to understand what happened? Why she died? Why?'

She took a long time to answer, as if she was checking back over her daughter's twenty or so years of life, day by day, before deciding. The deep brown eyes opened wide as she looked at me. 'Yes, I believe she would.'

'Then tell me two things—first, about the work.'

'It was political. They were compiling dossiers, on film, on people they . . . disliked.'

'People like Marjorie Legge and . . . who's that husband of hers?'

'Monty Porter,' she said automatically.

'Right, and Phil Broadhead?'

'I don't know actual names, but, yes, I think . . . people like that. Politicians too.'

'God,' I said. 'That's dangerous. Leo didn't know about this?'

'No.'

'So you must have suspected . . . you must have thought her death was connected to this work?'

'No.'

'No?'

'She was a filmmaker. She might have got something embarrassing on these people, but to kill her . . . ?'

'All right, all right. Yes, sure. Now, Carmel and de

Vries fought about this. What sorts of fights?'

'He was more radical than her, in every way. That's all I know. Surely you could have found out some of this from him.'

'He's disappeared.'

'What? Why?'

'His wife thought he had run off with Carmel.'

'That's ridiculous.' She realised what she'd said and a hesitant look appeared on her face. Her hands had unclenched as we'd talked but they turned back into fists again.

'Mrs Wise, do you know where Carmel and de Vries went to work and conduct their affair?'

Again a long silence. She was yielding up her knowledge and interpretation of her daughter piece by piece, and it was painful. 'Yes,' she whispered. 'I know.'

'Where? You must tell me.'

'They had a sort of studio in a house in Balmain. On the top floor.'

'Do you know the address?'

'It's 3A Grafton Street, near the water.'

I thought I knew the street and tried to picture it. Container wharf, fashionable terraces, townhouse development. 'You've been there?'

'No, Carmel told me.'

'Thank you. You *have* met Jan de Vries?'

'Yes.'

'What did you think of him?'

'Charming, but I didn't like him. I doubt if he'll tell you the truth.'

We got up simultaneously and she showed me out. I didn't see Leo. We didn't speak again except to say goodnight. Then she went back into the big, empty house.

20

SCOTT had the radio on a rock station. Some melodic and rhythmic sounds were just audible as I got into the car.

'Nice,' I said. 'Who's that?'

'Dire Straits.'

'Nice. Well, any suspicious characters?'

He straightened his slumped spine. The air in the cab was tobacco-free which showed remarkable restraint. 'How do you tell? Some people went past. Some looked, some didn't. I felt like I was standing in the middle of the SCG wearing a dress.'

I smiled; it was a bizarre image. 'That probably means no-one noticed you.' I wondered if I was telling the truth. The only way to check on whether anyone who is any good at it is watching you is to let yourself be watched, you can't do it by proxy.

'Where to now?'

'Balmain, and you can have a cigarette if you keep the window down and blow it out.'

'Right.' He started the taxi, checked that the hiring light was out and moved off. The lighted cigarette was in his fist within seconds. I checked for a tail but it's hard to do as a passenger. You get a different sense of things as a driver. I couldn't tell.

'Is anyone following us?' I said.

He shrugged. 'How would I know? I've never been in the movies before.'

I laughed and listened to some more Dire Straits on the radio. It was the best popular music I'd heard since early Van Morrison. I wondered what sort of music Carmel Wise liked. That set me off on thoughts of de Vries and Carmel Wise and their personal and working relationship. Judy Syme hadn't mentioned a place in Balmain and Barbara de Vries didn't know anything about it. It looked like the best bet as a bolt-hole for de Vries who was frightened of something. Frightened enough to stay away from his wife and kids and work for two weeks. Then the thought hit me for the first time. Maybe he wasn't staying away at all—maybe he was dead.

Darling Street was quiet but there looked to be a good deal of life in the pubs and coffee shops. There'd probably be some talk of films in there. Of books, too. Of books being turned into films and films being turned into books and everything being turned into reputation and reputation being turned into money. We reached East Balmain and made the turn. The streets drop sharply towards the container terminal and Galvani was driving on his brakes.

'Hold on!' I pressed a non-existent brake pedal; Scott braked sharply.

'What?'

'That's him! Stay back.'

I'd seen the face clearly by streetlight as the man had turned out of a lane and begun to tramp down towards the point. A stocky man, wearing a battle jacket and jeans. He was carrying a plastic bag and he flicked dark, straight hair back from his eyes as he made the turn. I saw the drooping moustache and the thrusting jaw. The jaw was bristled with an almost-beard but the man was unmistakably Jan de Vries.

The taxi was barely rolling. 'What'd we do?' Scott whispered.

'Pull in. I know where he's going. Let him get a bit further ahead and drive on around there.' I pointed ahead; the street ran down to the fence surrounding the container dock and then turned sharp left. There was a townhouse complex at the point of the turn—a cluster of sloping tile roofs and brown bricks that occupied a prime site right on the water. We watched de Vries until he'd made the turn and then Scott drove in the same direction; he turned, past de Vries who was going uphill now, and continued on, to where the street ended at the entrance to another waterfront site undergoing development. There had been a half-hearted attempt to close the site off with metal pickets but the residents had knocked them down and were still parking there as they always had.

'Hop in there,' I said. 'And switch off. Can you turn off the interior light?'

'Sure.' Scott clicked it off and I got out of the cab. It was dark in the street although there seemed to be distant light all around—from the city over the water and the houses higher up on the point. I squinted down the hill and saw de Vries toiling along until he suddenly stepped out of sight, through the gate of one of the big, old terrace houses overlooking the new townhouses which had grabbed the waterfront.

'I'm going in to talk to him.' I let the car door close quietly.

'You think there'll be trouble?'

'Could be. I won't start it. If he won't let me in I'll wait till he comes out. I don't want to push it.'

'Could he sneak out the back?'

'Not usually, not from the top floor. But you could take a wander around if you like. Did you see him?'

'Yeah. Looked like a wrestler.'

'I doubt it. Well, should know something soon.'

Negotiating an old, inner city footpath with one eye in the dark is no picnic. I stumbled along, almost missed the gutter and had to grab a fence for

152

support once or twice. Anyone seeing me could be forgiven for thinking I was drunk. A car turned into the street and drove purposefully past the terraces. I caught a glimpse of the number 3 on a letter box and pushed the gate beside it open. The rickety paling fence had 3A and an arrow painted on it in crude scrawl. The arrow pointed up the side of the house to a set of steps like a fire-escape. Wrong again, Hardy, there *was* a back way out.

Number 3 Grafton Street was in reasonable condition; it had been painted not too long ago and the weeds jutting up from the path had been cut fairly recently. At the rear, however, things were not so good. The back of the house featured some decayed plumbing and a gully-trap that smelled like a sewer. There were several bright lights shining inside on the top floor, as if for a party, but the only sound I could hear was from a turned-down TV set. The light was enough to show me the bottom step and let me get a grip on the handrail to make the ascent. The steps were steep and far apart; I jarred my eye misjudging the distance on the first few.

I stood outside the door on a small platform high above ground level. The platform's low rail had come away from the wall; the platform itself creaked. I felt like a trapeze artist. The resident could deal very effectively with Seventh Day Adventists and other unwelcome visitors. It was a doorstep to keep your temper on. I knocked. No answer.

'Dr de Vries.'

A scuffling noise or maybe nothing at all.

'I saw you go in, Dr de Vries. I've identified you from a photograph your wife gave me. I got the address here from Carmel's mother. I'm working for her father.' I felt foolish talking to myself up there. I had to *do* something. I bent and put the photograph and my licence under the door and gave them a

153

shove. 'This is the photo from your house and these are my credentials. If you've got a phone there you could ring Leo Wise and check on me.'

Now I definitely heard movement inside. I pictured him creeping across and picking up the photo and licence folder. It was like trout fishing. What other bait did I have? I remembered that I still had Leo Wise's cheque in my wallet. Under the door with it. 'That's all I've got, Dr de Vries. I think I know what your trouble is. You'd be well advised to talk to me.'

'Are you alone out there?' The American voice was shaky and uncertain, not the way American voices usually sound.

'Yes.'

'Stand back against the rail. The door opens out. I've got a rifle here and I'll shoot you if you make a wrong move.'

'Fair enough. I'm back as far as I can go. Hurry up, will you? This thing's bloody unsafe.'

The door opened and de Vries stood framed against the bright light. He was broad and thick and even from five feet away I could smell the whisky on his breath.

'I don't have a rifle,' he said.

'You don't need one. Let me come in. Maybe we can help each other.'

He nodded and stepped aside. I walked through the whisky fumes into a large room that must have had five hundred watts burning in it. A couple of double mattresses formed a low bed in one corner; a TV set and VCR plus a big console and screen all covered with switches and blinking lights occupied the middle of the room and there were some chairs, books and clothes scattered about. The whisky bottle and a glass were on top of the TV. I took the photo and the papers away from de Vries. He surrendered them without protest and walked across to the bottle.

'Join me?'

I shook my head. 'It's not the answer.'

'What is?'

'Do you know who killed Carmel?'

He shook his head and took a big slug of Bell's.

'Do you know why she was killed?'

'I guess so.'

'You were compiling a sort of dossier on the movers and shakers, that right?'

'Who told you that?'

'Carmel's mother.'

'Shit,' he said. 'I hope nobody else talks to her. I thought it was just Carmel and me and . . .'

'Who else? Who knows?'

He glanced fearfully at the door which he hadn't quite shut. Then he drank again. 'Whoever killed her.'

'What sort of stuff did she have?'

'Hot. Shots of people meeting wrong people. She used special mikes and picked up conversations.'

'Didn't you know how dangerous that was?'

'It was her idea.'

'I was told you were the more radical one.'

He shrugged. 'I had the . . . manipulative ideas but Carmel had the concept.' He snorted and emptied his glass. 'Listen to me. I'm talking like a movie producer.' He reached for the bottle and poured another big drink. He was drunk but a long way from incapable. Still, I thought I'd make that his last even if I had to use the .38 to convince him.

'You'll have to make that clearer.'

He drank again, flicked back the hair and leaned towards me intently. 'Look, you have to understand that she was the most brilliant kid with film I've ever seen, or heard of.'

'I've seen *Bermagui*.'

'Nothin'. He snapped his fingers. 'Nothin', to what she could do. What she did with this footage was amazing—the way she cut it and laid in the con-

155

versations and did the voice-overs. Devastating.'

'Who did she film—Legge and Porter, Broadhead . . .'

'Yeah, and others. Carmody, Gabriani . . .'

'Jesus.' Wal Carmody was a renegade policeman who advertised himself as a 'security consultant'; Carlo Gabriani owned stud farms and helicopters—a few years back he'd owned market gardens and a couple of broken-down trucks. 'What was the idea?'

'Expose the lot. Get film and sound showing they interconnect, how they meet. They meet in parks a lot, you know that? So they can't be bugged. Didn't stop Carmel, amazing judgement on where to put a mike. She could bug a phone, a room . . .'

'Have you done any of that?'

'A bit.'

'Whose places?'

'I'm not sure. I got scared and I wanted to back away but Carmel kept getting braver.'

More whisky went down. The only reason I had to believe that he was lying was Moira Wise's view that de Vries was the more radical, but that's what I did believe. 'Her mother thinks you were pushing her.'

He sneered. 'Push that chick? Push the Opera House—same result.'

'What did you mean by manipulative ideas?'

His head dropped forward and I thought he was going to let go of his glass, but, trust a drunk, that's the last thing they'll do. His shoulders shook and I realised he was crying. Maybe he was drunker than I'd thought. The sobbing became louder and his shoulders jerked compulsively. Fat bulged at the waistline under the T-shirt and his thighs strained the stitching of his jeans. It was hard to be patient with him; I had the feeling that he was crying not for Carmel, but for himself. I took the glass away and slapped him lightly. 'What did you mean, Dr de Vries?'

156

He lifted his head and looked at me with shocked eyes. 'You hit me.'

'Just barely. Manipulative ideas—what does that mean?'

His smile was loose and foolish. 'We ... she sent some samples.'

'You bloody idiot. Pull yourself together! Who did you send them to?'

He gulped and wiped his eyes. Another gulp and he was steadier. 'I don't know. Carmel kept the records. Brilliant ... ' he drank and spilled some of the whisky out of the corner of his mouth,' ... brilliant.'

'What're you saying?'

'Know what she did? You'll love this. She dropped the footage of the targets, the meetings and all, into commercial videos and tapes from the TV. Off-line edits. Same with the records—dates, names. All on tape. All in the middle of movies.' He laughed. 'Crazy chick.'

'These samples. What were they?'

'Just bits of film—highlights.'

'That was your idea, to send this stuff to the people. Why?'

'Push the bastards! Push 'em!' The drink was giving him a spurt of aggression. 'Worked too. Ran around like crazy things. Carmel got this shot of ... well, I won't say who it was ... with this hit man. Got 'em, right there. On film.'

'You maniac! One of them killed her, you know that?'

He nodded. 'Nearly killed me too. Why d'you think I'm here?' He emptied his glass and reached for the bottle. He was slow and sluggish and I beat him to it. I had the bottle by the neck and would've liked to brain him with it.

'What happened?'

'Drink.'

'After. What happened? You weren't at the Green-

157

wich?'

He shook his head. 'I was at the car. Guy took a shot at me. I ran.'

'Did you see him?'

A floorboard creaked and there was a sudden draught smelling of cement and the sea. 'You saw me, didn't you, de Vries?' A man came through the door. Two things about him frightened me. One was the gun in his hand, the other was that he was tall and thin with dark, unruly hair and a broken nose—just like me.

21

THE resemblance didn't seem to strike de Vries or the man with the gun as forcibly as it did me. But then, they didn't know what I looked like without the eye-pad. The gun was a real show-stopper—smallish calibre and with a silencer fitted. That meant the user was a good shot who was prepared to come up close to his work.

'Move a bit, Hardy,' he said. 'He goes first.'

'No!' de Vries shrieked. 'No, no!' He held the glass in front of his face and put his free hand up with the fingers spread.

'Yes,' the man said. He moved forward quickly, brought the gun up and fired twice. The glass exploded with a sound louder than the two pops from the gun. Fragments bounced against the wall and the TV set. De Vries' head dropped forward and his dark hair was suddenly made darker by the welling, spurting blood. The gun swung towards me. I had no chance to reach for the .38 under my jacket. There was just no point. He tensed his arm and then suddenly relaxed it a fraction.

'Jesus,' he said. 'It's like shooting my fuckin' self.'

'How did you find him?' I moved a millimetre; if he'd let me move maybe I could fall off the chair and move some more. If he'd let me live that long.

'Picked you up at the Lane Cove house, Hardy. Been following you from there.'

'Not you, someone else.'

'Right.' He seemed transfixed by the resemblance between us. He stared at me. If I'd had a watch on a chain I could've mesmerised him. 'He's gone to pass on the news about the videos.'

'You were listening?'

'Yeah, Jesus, this is uncanny.' He had a thick New Zealand accent which muffled the vowels.

'What's your name?' I had a mad desire to know the name of the man who was going to kill me.

'Doesn't matter, mate. You're dead.' The words seemed to release him from the trance. He tensed again.

'Who do you work for?'

'Forget it, Hardy. Time to go. You want to turn around?'

Time to move, I thought. Move! Go! I hurled myself sideways and heard a shattering sound of metal on glass. I was on the floor. My eye felt as if it had been torn out of the socket. I heard the sound again, louder. The silenced gun popped twice and the TV set exploded above me as I rolled for non-existent cover. I had the .38 in my hand and I fired wildly, missing the gunman by ten feet. The window was broken and a big metal garbage tin was rolling on the floor.

My lookalike stepped clear of the bin and skidded on broken glass as he tried to draw a bead on me.

'Look out!' I screamed at nothing and nobody. The shot I'd fired had hurt my eye; it sounds crazy but that's how it felt. The *sound* had hurt. I was ready to hurt it again, but I wasn't going to get the chance. He'd steadied like a professional and had the gun level and just slightly tracking me as I rolled. I bumped into the wall and things went loose inside my head. Then his gun jammed. He scrabbled at it, tore at the silencer. I fired at him and missed. I fired again and the bullet hit somewhere and staggered him. He spun around and ran for the door.

160

It seemed to take me an age to get to my feet. De Vries' blood had soaked and spread through the sea-grass matting and I slipped on a patch of it on the way to the door. I had to grab the door to steady myself before I could attempt the steps. I could hear panting and scuffling below me and the sound of feet slapping on the wooden steps.

'Cliff ... you all right?' It was Galvani, yelling from below but also doing something else.

'Yes.' I started down the steps, hugging the wall.

'He's getting away,' Galvani yelled. 'Hurry.'

I hurried as much as my bad vision and thundering head would let me. At the bottom of the steps Galvani had a man pinned to the ground, his face slammed into a pile of garbage that had been emptied out of a tin.

'He went that way!' Galvani pointed towards the waterfront units at the end of the street. 'Fuck you!' Galvani hammered the squirming man's head down into the garbage.

'Can you hold him?' I said. I was panting for breath, squinting and trying to get clearer vision.

'I can dislocate his arms.'

'No!' The man screamed. 'Kelly, help me, you bastard.'

'Hold him,' I said. 'I'll get the other one.'

I ran towards the street with pain splitting my head apart. Lights were coming on in the houses and people were shouting out of their windows. I saw Kelly ahead, running in a staggering, weaving motion towards the units. I lumbered after him with the gun in my hand and no chance at all of hitting anything smaller than a semi-trailer.

Kelly looked back, stopped and made another attempt to free the mechanism of his gun. He failed and threw the thing away. I gained on him although it was painful, uphill work. By the time he reached the low brick fence surrounding the units, my good

161

eye had cleared and I thought I might get a shot at him against the backdrop of the white painted apartment block. I stopped and raised the gun.

'Stop!' I shouted.

He lunged forward and vaulted the fence. I sighted, expecting to see his dark shape, but there was nothing but a short, piercing scream, a thud like a collision on a football field and a loud splash. I stood in the middle of the steep, narrow road and lowered my gun. I became aware of the sounds around me: voices, dogs howling, doors slamming and, far off but getting closer, the wail of a police siren.

The uniformed men happily responded when I told them to call Mercer or Drew. They didn't want any part of it and contented themselves with calming the residents and putting calls through to the meat wagon and the forensic people. They put Scott Galvani's prisoner, a plump man with a brave moustache and frightened eyes, in their car, and stood around sceptically waiting for the detectives.

I had time for a few words with Scott Galvani before they came.

'Thanks,' I said. 'I'd be dead if you hadn't chucked that tin in. What happened?'

Galvani had a cigarette going and his hands were shaking. We were standing at the point where Kelly had vaulted over the fence. Below, a long way down, he was wedged into the narrow, rocky cleft of the drainage ditch that ran down towards the water. From the position of the body it looked as if he'd gone in head first and it was too long a fall to survive. If he'd made his jump six feet to the left he'd have landed on the grassy bank in front of the units. Galvani drew deeply on the cigarette. 'It was so confusing. I can hardly remember. I did a bit of a prowl around the place. I didn't see them arrive. Must've been around the back then. Anyway, this guy,' he
162

indicated the man in the police car, 'he goes to the phone just around the corner. I saw the other one, he'd been listening up there, outside the door, he pulls out a gun and goes in. I went and threw the garbage bin. Thought that might give you a chance with your gun.'

'It did. Sort of.'

'The other one came back and I clobbered him. After that, you know, you saw it all.'

'Yeah. You say he made a phone call?'

'That's right.'

'Bugger it. There goes the evidence.' I walked over to the car and looked at the bulky man. I made window-winding gestures and he put the window down.

'Who d'you work for, son?'

He clenched his soft jaw and thought about it. When he'd worked it out he said, 'I work for Kev . . . Kev Kelly.'

'You're unemployed. Who'd you ring?'

The jaw clenched again and this time he didn't speak. 'Give him a cigarette, Scott. You don't object, officer?'

The cop shook his head. 'Where's that fuckin' Mercer?'

'He'll be along.'

The man took the cigarette and jutted his head out the window for Galvani to light it. He puffed and still didn't say anything.

'It could be your ace in the hole,' I said. 'Or it could be your death warrant. You know Kelly killed two people? One tonight and a girl a couple of weeks ago?'

'I wasn't there for that.'

'No? Well, it'll be interesting to see how you go. Good luck.' The cop wound the window up and the man's face looked even rounder and more pale through the glass.

A car pulled up and Drew got out. He slouched

163

across towards me with his hands in his pockets.

'Well?'

I pointed to the wall. 'Over there you've got the man who killed Carmel Wise.'

He walked to the wall and looked down. 'Who says so?'

'I do.'

'Witnesses?'

'Sort of.' I was thinking of Judy Syme and Michael Press. They could testify to Kelly's earlier visit to the Randwick flat. Maybe Ellen Barton from the flats near the Greenwich Apartments could identify him. Maybe. It was thin.

An ambulance and another car arrived. The uniformed men spoke briefly to Drew and began to direct some of the troops towards the house, and others to the drainage ditch.

'Who've we got inside?' Drew said. We walked along the street which was ablaze with light. Windows and doors were open; radios were playing. 'And who's this?' Drew jerked his thumb at Galvani.

I told him about de Vries and his connection with Carmel Wise. I described Scott as my 'assistant' which brought a laugh from Drew. He seemed careless and uninterested but in fact he was looking keenly at everything. It was him who spotted the gun with the silencer in the gutter. He bent and examined it.

'Kelly's,' I said. 'He used it on de Vries. Then it jammed before he could do me.'

'Pity,' Drew said. 'You got a gun?'

I took it from the holster and gave it to him. 'There'll be one bullet in Kelly somewhere. One or two others in the room upstairs.'

'One or two?' Drew said.

'I'm not in the best condition for shooting.' I touched the eye pad. The pain had subsided to a dull

164

ache. I had the drops in my pocket and the pain-killers but I wouldn't give Drew the satisfaction.

'You did all right,' he said. 'Wait here. I'll take a look upstairs.'

Scott and I leaned against a car parked outside number 3. He smoked and I used the eyedrops. There were no lights on in the ground level of the house. Glass from the broken window littered the lawn. Gradually, lights went out in the houses. The ambulance and police lights stopped blinking and the street became quieter, except at the top where a team was working to raise Kelly's body.

'Wouldn't mind a drink,' Scott said.

'Me too. We'll probably get some coffee from the coppers.'

'Eh?'

'I thought you watched TV. Statements, mate. Waiting around for the police to fill in forms. That's what this job is all about.'

'You told me it was about visiting people and look what happened.'

'Busy night,' I said. De Vries' body was carried on a stretcher by two bearers who struggled on the steep stairs. Drew came after them. Galvani stared at the covered shape on the stretcher. Blood had already soaked through the blanket where the head would be. He turned away while they loaded the stretcher into the ambulance. Then he lit another cigarette and yawned.

'I'm tired.'

'Forget it,' I said. 'The night is young. Isn't it, Drew?'

22

GALVANI and I travelled to the city in the taxi. I told him to turn the meter on but he wouldn't. His driving was just as good as it had been before. Mercer showed up at Headquarters to grab some of the action. Drew organised some coffee for Galvani and me and some more cigarettes. Everyone did nothing for a while, then we gave our statements to a stenographer. I read mine over and signed it. Scott did the same.

'Are you going to call Helen?' he said.

I shook my head. 'She's at a friend's place. I'll tell her all about it tomorrow.'

'It *is* tomorrow.'

We were in a bare room with a couple of chairs and a table, a blackboard on an easel and harsh fluorescent light. The diagram on the blackboard looked like a stakeout but it could have been the plans for the Commissioner's new office. Mercer wandered in with the statements in his hand. He perched on the table and looked at me. I took two more pain-killers with the dregs of my coffee.

'Big names, Hardy,' he said. 'And big guesses. If all this is right how'd the . . . what d'you call them, targets, know it was Wise who sent the stuff?'

'She was so good that she might just as well have signed her name on it. Do you reckon people like Porter and Gabriani can't find out who the hot film-makers around town are?'

He grunted. 'But no proof.'

'That's right. What does the other guy say?'

'Nothing, except to ask me to get his lawyer—Richard Riddell.'

The name had been in the papers. 'That's Carmody's lawyer.'

He nodded. 'And Monty Porter's. That doesn't get us anywhere.'

'Will you contact Riddell?'

'In the morning. I'm working on a charge. It's a little tricky.'

'What've you got on the late Kelly?'

'A bit. Enzedder, a pro. They tell me he looked a lot like you. Some relation?'

'Not that I know of.'

'Wouldn't surprise me. Well, I suppose you and your mate . . .'

He broke off as the door opened abruptly and a uniformed constable stuck his head in. 'Sergeant.'

'What?'

The Constable beckoned Mercer over and whispered to him. Mercer nodded and closed the door. 'More fun and games,' he said.

'Let me guess. Somebody called at the Greenwich Apartments tonight and took away all the movies.'

Mercer smiled. 'Wrong. Somebody torched the whole place. Want to take a look?'

I thanked Galvani again, told him to go home and that I'd see him again soon. 'If you're serious about the security business I'll write you a reference,' I said.

'Sure. Well, it was interesting.'

'We'll have a drink. I owe you money too.'

'You don't.'

'I'll bill the client, so I'll have to pay you.'

We shook hands and he left.

Drew drove and Mercer and I sat in the car and didn't say anything. There were still a few

167

optimistic and strong-legged girls on the beat up William Street, but the traffic was light and the city noise had settled into its 24-hour, 365-day-a-year hum. I ran the whole business over in my mind for missed opportunities and bad luck. I should have checked carefully to see whether I was being followed—not driving and only having one eye were no excuse. If I could've had a clear go at de Vries, things would have been different. I thought back to the Greenwich Apartment flat where I'd played a bit of *The Running Man*. I closed my eyes and saw the action—the figures on the boat, heads together. I don't have great recall of movies but I'd suffered this one twice and knew it pretty well. The scene I'd played didn't belong in the movie. I'd seen some of Carmel Wise's work without knowing it.

'How long had de Vries been screwing the video girl?' Mercer said.

'That's a stupid name for her.'

'Fits doesn't it? One way or another. How long?'

'I don't know. A couple of months. Why?'

'His wife took it bad.'

The fire was still burning when we got there. The upper floors had been scorched more than set ablaze but the ground floor was a blackened, shattered ruin. Tongues of flame still licked at the ivy, ran along a dry branch and then flickered out. The firemen were playing water on the walls and keeping an eye on the adjacent buildings.

We walked up as close to the entrance as we could but the heat kept us back twenty feet or more. Smoke billowed out of flat one—dense, stinking clouds of it and there were popping noises and sharp cracks as if fireworks were going off.

Mercer stepped across to talk to the fireman who seemed to be doing the most shouting and the least work. I went with him.

168

'Police,' Mercer said.

'Yes?'

'Deliberate?'

The man snorted. He was stocky and red-faced naturally; in the glow from the fire he seemed to be alight himself. 'One hundred per cent. Professional job.'

'How's that?'

The fireman took off his hard hat and mopped his face. 'No-one hurt. People had time to get clear. Looks like there was a sort of preliminary bang and then a couple of blasts. That's how the pros do it.'

'Any chance of anything intact in there?' I pointed to the ground floor flat.

'No way.'

I became aware of the people in the courtyard. Singly and in pairs they stood around, some fully dressed and some in nightwear. They watched the fire with fascination. There was a light breeze and the noxious smoke was lifted up between the buildings and blown away. The plane tree nearest the Greenwich Apartments was scorched; its leaves were brown and curling. A fine ash started to fall on the bricks.

'Mr Hardy!'

Ellen Barton came towards me; she was wearing a red silk dressing gown and enormous white slippers. Her purple hair was in disarray and I could see pink skull in patches where it was thin.

'Hello, Ellen,' I said.

'Whatever happened to your eye?'

'A long story. Did you see what happened here?'

Her head swivelled and her eyes opened. She sized Mercer and Drew up, probably guessed their ranks and years of service. 'I was asleep. That lovely building. What a shame. What'll happen to it now?'

'I don't know,' I said. Then I saw Leo Wise coming along the lane. He was walking slowly and

169

had a hat in his hand as if he'd taken it off out of respect for something or someone.

'Excuse me.' I nodded to Ellen Barton and went to meet Wise. Drew and Mercer watched me as I guided him to one of the benches in the courtyard. We sat and he looked at the smouldering building.

'This is to do with Carmel, of course,' he said.

'Yes.' I ran through it as quickly as I could. Mercer and Drew moved around restlessly. When I'd finished Wise looked away from the fire and stared at me.

'You're sure he was the one? This Kelly?'

'He virtually said so, but de Vries was the only witness.'

'It's good enough for me. Thanks, Hardy.'

'The building's a mess.'

He shrugged. 'It's insured. I can probably even claim on the the kid's videos.'

He wept then. I suspected that he hadn't cried much before but he let it all go now in great gulping sobs. I patted his shoulder; Mercer and Drew watched for a while, then they drifted off down the lane.

We sat there a long time. The sky lightened. The people went back into their flats when the firemen gave them the word. Water hissed on the fire and the smoke welled up again and again. A smell of wet ash wafted through the courtyard and hung in the air. Eventually Wise lifted his head and wiped his eyes.

'Christ,' he said, 'what a crazy thing for her to do. Will we ever know which one of the bastards was behind it?'

I shook my head. 'Probably not.'

'Crazy,' he said. 'Kids, they break your heart.'

'Yeah.' I put my hand up to my eye and eased the pressure of the pad. 'That's what my mother used to say.'

170

23

THE deaths of Jan de Vries and Kevin Kelly and the fire-bombing of the Greenwich Apartments got a pretty big coverage in the papers. They made the tie-in with 'the Video Girl' too—there was no way to stop that. But the pornographic angle didn't get a run.

The day following these events, Marjorie Legge and Monty Porter went on a world tour to study new markets for Australian products. When she was asked at the airport what products were involved Ms Legge turned to her husband and said, 'Monty?' Monty Porter punched the journalist on the nose.

About the same time, Carlo Gabriani left the country to investigate the distribution of Australian relief money to the victims of recent natural disasters in Italy. It was rumoured that he had some government backing for the trip, but that was only a rumour. I phoned Drew to ask him if he'd seen these interesting items in the press.

'Rich people fly around the world all the time,' he said. 'Wouldn't you?'

'I might. Don't you find the timing interesting?'

'Not really. It's coming on to winter here. Be lovely in the south of France about now. Probably be okay in Italy too. By the way, how's the eye?'

'I'm shocked, Drew. You've asked after my well-being.'

'Not really. I'm wondering how you'll look on the stand identifying people and all, when they point out you'd had an eye operation a couple of days before.'

'I saw well enough to hit Kelly.'

'Close range and you got him one out of four. It won't look good, Hardy.'

In fact the eye was fine. I went to see Stivens at the appointed time and he was impressed by my progress. I was impressed by his Macquarie Street rooms and the size of the bill.

'Two anaesthetists?' I said.

'Back up. In case one passes out.'

'You made a joke.'

'It's an old joke. I learned it from someone who explained it to me.'

You couldn't catch Mr Stivens out, no matter how hard you tried. He told me to keep using the drops and to discard the pad when I wasn't troubled by glare.

I charged Wise for one of the anaesthetists and for 50 per cent of the costs that weren't covered by Medicare. He paid promptly, which is an unusual thing for a rich man to do. I discarded the pad. I spent a lot of time in shaded bedrooms with Helen, doing it gently, and glare didn't bother me a bit.

Richard Riddell engaged the services of a barrister with no known connections to any of the people Carmel Wise had investigated, to represent Derek William Allen, who was charged as an accessory to the murder of de Vries. Allen died, apparently of a heroin overdose, while on bail and before the case came to trial.

The block of flats at Tamarama didn't have concrete cancer. Helen paid a deposit, the tenants moved out and she was in as a tenant herself, awaiting settlement, in a matter of weeks. I helped her to buy furniture and move her meagre belongings from my house to the flat. The first night we spent there the

172

place was bare and we ate and sat and slept like Spartans. But gradually, the place took shape. I found I liked travelling over there by train and foot, or driving late at night. Some nights Helen stayed at my place.

We swam at Bondi often, although temperatures were dropping and it was more a matter of getting wet briefly and getting warm quickly than of frolicking in the surf. We walked along the headlands, rambled in the cemetery, drank coffee in Bondi and wine in the pub at Coogee. It was a happy time without friction. Our six months were slipping by very fast.

I'd returned the cassette of *Bermagui* to Judy Syme with some regret, but a few weeks later the film was shown on television accompanied by the inevitable 'Video Girl' nonsense. Helen and I watched it in her flat. Carmel Wise had created a place where people collided, where some things were resolved and others were not and where the final story was never really told. Sometimes her camera panned out over the sea and up into the clouds as if the real solutions might be there which meant that they were nowhere at all. I stared at the dark water and the starry sky and thought that the partial understanding we'd got of why she'd died—and no answer at all to the question of who had ordered her death—was what she would have expected.

DEAL ME OUT
Peter Corris

Cliff Hardy starts out to help a friend but before long he's
looking for an enemy - William Mountain, boozer, TV
scriptwriter, would-be novelist, who is missing and
searching for adventure. Mountain's adventure is Hardy's
'case' which rapidly becomes a case he would rather not
have. The only good thing about Mountain is his girlfriend, Erica Fong, but before long she is in mortal
danger. Mountain is the dealer in a deadly game and
Hardy's cards are clues which take him from Woolloomooloo to Woollahra, and from the Blue Mountains to
Melbourne.

Hardy sticks to the trail as he must, but for Erica and for
his pride rather than the hundred and twenty five a day
and expenses. But the bodies and minds he meets
more and more unsound, and the hands Bill Mountain
deals become more and more bizarre...

THE BIG DROP
Peter Corris

A client happens to fall from the twentieth storey of a
building; a rock star goes missing; an erotic Mongol scroll
vanishes; a film star has a problem that has nothing to do
with creativity - it's all in a day's work for Cliff Hardy.
Yachts dance on the sparkling waters of the harbour, and
the back alleys are busy; the city's high and low classes go
about their daily business. But nothing really surprises
Hardy; and, for a hundred and twenty-five dollars a day (plus
expenses), he'll provide a few surprises of his own....

'Peter Corris is turning out some of the most entertaining
fiction in Australia today....'
The Age

Published by Unwin Paperbacks.

THE EMPTY BEACH
Peter Corris

It began as a routine investigation into a supposed drowning.
But Cliff Hardy, private detective, soon found himself
literally fighting for his life in the murky, violent underworld
of Bondi.

The truth about John Singer, black marketeer and poker
machine king, is out there somewhere - amidst the drug
addicts and prostitutes and alcoholics. Hardy's job is to stay
alive long enough in the world of easy death to get to

the truth.
The truth hurts...

'...a fine, tightly-controlled story.'
West Australian

Published by Unwin Paperbacks

HEROIN ANNIE
Peter Corris

Cliff Hardy in action again: trying to keep one step ahead of
his client's troubles - and his own.
He has to cope with the brute force exercised in sleazy back
streets to the more refined form of violence to be found in
the boardrooms of city skyscrapers. Along the way he has to
deal with everyone from fashion models and teenage
junkies to urban developers and crooked funeral directors.
Some are friendly and helpful, some try to kill him...
Hardy copes, with his guts and his savvy, and all for a
hundred and twenty-five dollars a day (plus expenses)...

Published by Unwin Paperbacks.

THE WINNING SIDE
Peter Corris

The Winning Side is a moving and compassionate account
of a man caught between two worlds.
Charlie Thomas, born in a humpy camp to Aboriginal
parents in the 1920's, learns to fight early. He fights in the
backblocks of Queensland during the Depression, and in
the Middle East and Pacific in World War Two.
As a decorated veteran, he fights on in the cities and the
country against racial prejudice, authority and his own
weaknesses. He has to fight; white Australia tries to keep
him on the losing side - in the boxing tents, pubs and gaols
Charlie Thomas fights for education, justice, hope and love
- to make his side the winning side.

Published by Unwin Paperbacks.

ROOM TO MOVE

Women's Short Stories

These thirty-two short stories have been selected by
Suzanne Falkiner to present a balanced collection of
modern writing by *Australian* women. They include a
selection of some of Australia's best known names (Jolley,
Astley, Zwicky) through to the most promising emerging
writers (Garner, Sperling, Viidikas, Grenville) and some of
the more avant garde and experimental of the new voices
(Inez Baranay, Jeri Kroll, Finola Moorhead). A proportion,
including those of Garner and Zwicky, have never been
published before. Most have had previous publication in
small magazines, and have been selected by their authors
as among those they most wish to perpetuate.

Published by Unwin Paperbacks.